To those of you who have survived the worst.

The Greenhouse Pane!

The Myriad Mysteries #4

Claire Logan

1

The Chicago sunshine was bright, crisp and still a bit cool. Mrs. Pamela Jackson stepped out onto the rooftop of the Myriad Hotel, two toy poodles beside her. As the elevator closed behind her, she unhooked the dogs from their leashes, allowing them to roam about and do their business.

Ahead lay the vast and impressive Hotel gardens, dozens of raised boxes tended by Chef Monsieur and his crew. Most days, Mrs. Jackson would come up to help. But she'd risen late that day, and Monsieur had already left for the kitchens to prepare the days' meals. But a few of the men still worked there, smiling and tipping their caps as they passed.

She lit a cigarette, strolling to the right and around the elevator shaft after the dogs. She passed a door marked "Stair", then took a few steps towards what she thought of as the "back" of the rooftop.

The right side of the rooftop held a swimming pool, surrounded on two sides by covered lounge chairs with small drink tables between them. A stand lay behind the row of chairs facing her, which later in the day would serve drinks. Tea tables and chairs sat nearby. Beside that was a covered cart which contained towel, swimming caps, and other items — in case guests had forgotten them.

Closer to the far banister lay a concierge stand with telephone. At this hour, no one manned it, but you could call down — or out — for anything you might need. A modest hut roofed in white tile lay just before the far banister, with doors for gentlemen and ladies to refresh themselves, change clothes, and shower.

A stunning huge greenhouse took up much of the left side of the rooftop. The greenhouse itself was made up in clear glass, separated by silver which had faded by old patina into gray. It was a masterful work, soaring well above the rest of the structures here.

Straight ahead, far beyond the greenhouse and pool area, lay the service elevators, only accessible by key. The men who passed her earlier waited there with their carts. Large double doors opened; the men disappeared inside.

Mrs. Jackson strolled up to the little dogs, who were sniffing the area beside the greenhouse doors. She smiled down at them. "Find anything?"

The little dogs, one black, the other a much smaller black-and-gold spotted pup, looked up at her, ears raised, wagging their fluffy tails.

Mrs. Jackson laughed. "I've no food for you, sillies. You just ate!"

The day was lovely, quiet, still. Mrs. Jackson strolled to her left, along the length of the greenhouse, to lean on the waist-high stone banister.

She gazed out over the Chicago skyline. The automobiles were specks, the trucks ants in the distance.

It was a beautiful day. Yet she felt melancholy.

Bessie had given birth just before the New Year. The Myriad's Head Clerk, Mr. Lee Francis, had picked out her black-and-gold spotted pup as a companion for his baby son. Spot, as they called her, would be going to her new home today.

The last of Bessie's puppies to leave them.

She ran her fingers over the two empty black leather leashes in her hand. When she'd found the toy poodle starving outside the front door to the Myriad, she'd had no idea how old the little dog was. How long would it be before Bessie left her, too?

A deep voice called out, "There you are!"

Mr. Hector Jackson walked up to her. A tall, very dark, and quite handsome man, he'd dressed for the day, wearing one of his gray tweeds.

She turned to her Mr. Jackson, glad to see him. "Here I am!"

He chuckled at that, taking her arm. Then he sobered. "I don't like you standing so close. Isn't it dangerous?"

"I asked about this when we first arrived. You can't see it unless you look up while out on our balcony, but Monsieur told me there's a landing just ten feet down. For safety to those below, in case one might accidentally drop something over the side. There's a ladder somewhere to fetch things. If one fell over, they'd get bruises. But serious injury would be unlikely."

"That's a relief." Mr. Jackson did sound relieved.

The couple strolled back the way she'd come, the little dogs following, then trotting ahead. As they walked, he asked, "And how fares the city? Has it behaved?"

She laughed. "As it ever does, I suppose." He always did know how to make her smile. "What brings you up here today?"

He stopped. "Two things. First, I wished to see you. The morning sun frames you in a most glorious light."

She felt herself blush.

"The other is this. It just arrived." He handed her an opened envelope containing an embossed card:

YOU ARE INVITED
TO A ROOFTOP GALA
To Honor the Esteemed Horace Rothmore
On the Thirtieth Anniversary
Of His Grand Green-House Creation
Please Join Us
Myriad Hotel Rooftops
The Thirteenth of May
At Half Past Seven
RSVP

Mrs. Jackson handed it back to him. "How exciting!" She'd never heard of the man before, but the idea of a party on the rooftops felt intriguing. "What does one wear to such a thing?"

He grinned. "Oh, I'm sure we can find you something suitable." He glanced over at their dogs, who were sniffing round the pool. "Come away from there. Bessie! Spot!" As the dogs returned, he said to Mrs. Jackson, "Breakfast should be set up by now."

"Oh! That sounds wonderful." Clipping the dogs onto their leashes, the four set off for the elevator.

While she waited in front of the carved Art Deco doors for their elevator to arrive, Mrs. Jackson listened to Mr. Jackson's plans for the day. They sounded quite extensive! Breakfast in their suite, then shopping, out for lunch with their friends Ophelia Denton and George Neuberg, then a visit to the gardens at Grant Park. They'd come back to the Hotel to leave Spot with her new family, then dress for dinner and dancing.

At the end of all this, he said, "We shall keep you well-entertained."

"My word. And what's the occasion?"

He gave her a warm, fond smile. "Well, dear girl, if **you** can't think of it, I'll not spoil it by telling."

That seemed fair enough.

When the lovely doors opened, the couple and their dogs entered the rosewood-paneled elevator. The uniformed elevator man, a different one than had brought her up there, tipped his hat. "All the way, or just to your floor?"

"Just our floor, thank you," Mr. Jackson said. "We'd have gone down the stair, but that door at the top's been jammed a week now."

"They should have fixed the lock by now," the man said. "If I see Eugene, I'll send him up to look at it."

Eugene did all the "dirty work" around the place. But to be perfectly honest, there was no "they" — other than a few temporary hired hands for big jobs, he was one man in his early thirties caring for an enormous hotel. It wasn't surprising that he hadn't gotten to it.

Although to Mrs. Jackson, it sounded as if they hadn't yet told him of the problem.

The elevator doors opened. The hallways at the Myriad were splendid: tan marble floors, rosewood paneled walls, with brass fixtures casting lovely golden light. The suite doors had been painted to match the flooring and trimmed in brass. Lovely scenes of the city and lake guided them to their suite: 3205.

The couple entered through the door to Mr. Jackson's room. As they did, the smell of ham, eggs, and fried potatoes wafted out.

Will and Floyd glanced up when they came inside. Will was a pale fellow with light brown hair; Floyd was a slender young man almost as dark-skinned as her Mr. Jackson, though not nearly so tall.

Will was just setting their plates. "There you are!" He placed a plate with two small meaty bones on the table.

Floyd brought out a teapot and a small coffeepot, and began pouring their drinks.

Mrs. Jackson knelt to unhook her dogs' leashes. "You're up early!"

Mr. Jackson said, "Will, I almost forgot. Congratulations on your new position!"

Will had just been promoted to Assistant Head Waiter, and would be helping the Myriad's Head Waiter — their friend George Neuberg — oversee the waitstaff.

Freed from their leashes, the dogs ran to sniff out every corner of the suite.

Will beamed. "Thank you, sir."

Mr. Jackson held her jacket, and Mrs. Jackson slipped out of it and her shoes with a sigh. She so loved the feeling of the thick soft carpet.

"I'm just filling in," Will said. "I have the evening off. My family and I are driving to Oak Park for dinner."

Mr. Jackson said, "Oh? What's the occasion?"

"It's my grandmother's birthday."

Mrs. Jackson said, "How wonderful!"

Mr. Jackson handed each them a tip."Please give your grandmother our regards."

"Thanks! Glad to," said Will.

Floyd said, "Enjoy your breakfast." He pushed his cart out, and after looking round for the dogs, Will carefully closed the door behind them.

The couple sat side by side around the small round table, perhaps a foot apart. She sat to his right, as she'd always done, even with her first husband. Mrs. Jackson felt comfortable, safe. It was pleasant, eating beside the dear companion she'd grown to care for.

The food was delicious: the ham, faintly sweet and spicy, the potatoes fried with herbs, the eggs fixed just how she liked them. "Dear Monsieur," she said fondly. "He knows exactly my tastes." Then she chuckled to herself as she cut the ham's rind into small pieces. "I suppose he must, with as long as I've known him."

Mr. Jackson swallowed a bite. "Very true."

Bessie and Spot had stationed themselves by her chair, tails wagging, their faces upturned and expectant. She chuckled at them, setting the treat between them.

As they all ate, Mrs. Jackson puzzled over the mystery of their special day. Mr. Jackson had planned out everything!

But why? What was the occasion? Was it a holiday? "Let me see the newspaper, if you please."

He handed it over; she opened it.

The headlines were the usual scandals of the day. Inside the first page was much the same.

On the second page, the advertisements began. These were her favorite part — she liked to see what the women here were wearing, so she might best blend in.

It would certainly help when out shopping for this rooftop affair.

So many styles! And most of the newest sported skirts which showed much too much of the lower leg, and without a hint of a sleeve!

The styles seemed daring in the extreme, so different than what she was used to back home.

But she needed to fit in if she were to live here.

Finally she found a velvety dress with long sleeves, with a skirt draping almost to the ankle. She showed it to Mr. Jackson. "I think I'd like this, but in green."

"Oh," he said, "That'd be lovely." He peered at the paper. "We'll go there first."

She turned the page and found what looked like a society section.

A library tour. An astronomy meeting. A charity luncheon. Some heiress named Lydia Rothmore Von Bilten was starting a garden club.

Mrs. Jackson had wanted one day to find a place where she could have a garden of her own. Where puppies could run freely.

The thought made her smile.

Maybe she'd join this garden club. She'd learned about gardening from her mother, and learned much more from working with Monsieur here at the Hotel, growing food for the Myriad's tables. But it would be nice to meet other ladies with similar interests.

The rooftop gala wasn't even mentioned. Strange, that. But perhaps it was a private affair.

She folded the paper, began to eat. But the mystery of what her Mr. Jackson's plans might be about tickled at her mind.

Today seemed an ordinary spring day. Rather like —

She set her fork down. Instead of images of their first day in town, the shopping and ride to the hotel they now stayed in, she recalled the face of her first husband the night before that, as he lay dying.

"I'm sorry," Mr. Jackson said. "I'd hoped we might at least make it through breakfast."

Mrs. Jackson leaned her elbow on the table, her forehead upon her hand, just trying to breathe. Her beloved lying there, his last words echoing in her mind ... time had dulled the pain, but it was fierce still.

Bessie trotted over beside her, laying her soft little head upon Mrs. Jackson's foot.

She felt Mr. Jackson's hand, warm on hers. "You don't have to face it alone. We can get through this."

She nodded, the pain still too much to answer. Then she squeezed his hand, just a little. Took a deep breath. "Thank you."

He smiled at that, taking up her left hand to kiss it. The ring he'd given her glinted in the morning's light: a raised silver band with a clear stone set smoothly into it. "He did the right thing. Were I in his place, I might have done the same."

She turned her face to look at him, forehead still leaning on her hand. "And yet he died for it."

Mr. Jackson let out a breath. "That's the way of it sometimes. But it's worse to live with regret." He glanced aside. "Much worse."

She straightened, curiosity overcoming her pain. "What is it you regret?"

He shrugged. "Most of my decisions have been poorly done." Then he smiled, kissing her hand. "But not this one."

Then the reason behind his planning came to her. "Happy anniversary, my dear."

He gave her a fond smile. "Happy anniversary to you as well."

2

The couple went shopping for clothes, and Mrs. Jackson found the exact dress she wanted. Once they'd found a bright green bow for Bessie to wear on her collar at the gala, they met for lunch with their friends George Neuberg and Ophelia Denton at an outdoor café near Grant Park.

The couple had arrived at the cafe early, but for some reason their two friends showed up late. Even so, Mrs. Jackson was well-pleased to see them.

George was a tanned, dark-haired fellow, the Headwaiter at the Myriad Hotel. Ophelia was about Mrs. Jackson's height, with strawberry-blonde curls, and worked as a dance girl at Club Patruni. Ophelia wore the new dark mustard-colored hat and coat Mrs. Jackson had bought her for the holidays, and she looked gorgeous.

Blushing, Ophelia gave her a hug; George and Mr. Jackson warmly shook hands.

George and Ophelia both smiled, yet their smiles seemed strained.

"Let's go in," Mr. Jackson said. "We have a big day ahead of us."

"Sounds good," George said.

As they followed the waiter to their seats, Mrs. Jackson said, "We saw Will this morning. How's the training been?"

George chuckled. "It'll be nice to take an actual vacation once in a while."

"That does sound good," Mr. Jackson said.

The waiter stopped. "Your table." It was a lovely white wire table with four matching chairs and a large blue-and-white striped umbrella covering it.

The four of them sat. The waiter handed over their menus and left. George gestured to the dogs. "How's our little family?"

Mrs. Jackson chuckled. "I think we're all well. Giving Spot an outing before she ventures to her new home."

Ophelia beamed at the little gold and brown dog, leaning down to ruffle the pup's fur. "You'll get to run in a real yard!"

Mrs. Jackson sighed. It seemed unfair to be parted from the last of the little dogs she'd grown to love. But equally unfair to have growing pups cooped up in a hotel suite. They barely had room for Bessie.

Would she ever see Spot again?

I'm being silly, she decided. She got to see Bessie's golden-haired puppy almost every day.

Mr. Jackson took her hand. "I hope the both of you are well."

Ophelia gave a little half-shrug. "My friend Ethel's just been turned out of our boarding house." Ophelia turned to George. "That's why I was late meeting you."

Mrs. Jackson said, "Whatever for?"

"She was caught with a man behind the theater," Ophelia said. "Mrs. Kilpatrick was furious! She said she'd not run a house for loose women." Ophelia's shoulders drooped. "Her mother took her home."

"I'm sorry," Mrs. Jackson said. "What will she do?"

Ophelia shrugged. "Find a new job, unless she can get a place to stay here in town."

They sat for a moment, silent.

The waiter approached. "Are you ready to order?"

Ophelia chose a chicken salad, George ordered a club sandwich, Mrs. Jackson chose grilled fish, and Mr. Jackson ordered a plate of spaghetti with meat sauce. They also ordered tea, except for Mr. Jackson, who asked for coffee with heavy cream. Mrs. Jackson also ordered a glass of water.

"I've not been here before," said Mr. Jackson. "But Mr. Carlo recommended the place to me."

Mrs. Jackson thought that sounded good. But neither Ophelia nor George seemed cheered by this.

Ophelia was barely one and twenty, and she'd been close with Ethel. But what might be going on with George? She said to him, "Are your parents well?"

He shrugged, glancing away.

The waiter returned, setting out their drinks. After pulling their little dogs out of the way of the waiter, Mrs. Jackson said to Mr. Jackson, "This place has remarkably good service!"

The waiter smiled to himself and left.

She poured her water into a saucer and placed it on the ground for the dogs. Once they were done drinking, she fastened their leashes so they might not move too far from her chair. "I'll have something for you to eat soon."

The little dogs wagged their tails, ears up.

The day was beautiful, without wind, or even a cloud in the sky. People passed, and birds fluttered by.

But Mr. Jackson seemed lost in thought, George and Ophelia, glum.

Finally, the food arrived. "Oh!" Mrs. Jackson said. "This smells delicious."

The others perked up, nodding their agreement.

After checking carefully for any bones in her filet, she chopped a third of the large filet onto the dogs' saucer. When she placed the saucer back on the ground, Spot and Bessie set to eating at once.

Her grilled fish was cooked perfectly, with a savory lemon and herb sauce and a lovely crisp skin.

While they ate, Mrs. Jackson watched George. He spoke little, picking at his food.

About half-way through their meal, Ophelia said, "Off to powder my nose!"

Mrs. Jackson smiled at her. "And such a lovely nose it is, Pet."

Ophelia giggled, blushing.

Mr. Jackson rose. "I'll be right back."

The day was bright, with not a cloud in the sky. Mrs. Jackson gazed over at George as she sipped her tea. "You seem positively morose."

George sighed. "My father wanted to have 'a talk' over breakfast."

"Oh, dear."

George snorted. "Yeah. Apparently, it's 'high time you settled down'. By which he means married, preferably chained to his business somehow." George's father built yachts, and here on the shores of Lake Michigan had a thriving business among the well-to-do of Chicagoland.

"Can he **force** you to?"

This seemed to calm him. "Well, no. But I overheard my mother crying. She asked my dad what's going to become of me. She said things like, 'am I never getting grandchildren?' and 'what did we do wrong?'. I think they feel a failure because of me."

"I'm sorry."

"I can't fit myself into the life they want. Don't get me wrong: I love boats. Even making them, the sanding and building. But sitting at a desk all day, running a business ... it would drive me mad."

This sparked a memory of something her Mr. Jackson said once, long ago. She felt quite amused. "We shall have no madness here!"

He chuckled. Then his face sober. "And then last week it was Mr. Davis."

She had to stop a moment to recall who the man was, and it must have showed, because George said, "The Myriad Hotel's manager?"

"Oh," Mrs. Jackson said. "Yes."

"He's getting on, and he wants to split the duties so he doesn't have to see the customers. He wants to focus on the finances, let someone else take care of the front of house business." George shrugged. "I thought it ideal, and I even applied. But Mr. Carlo wouldn't hear of it.

He said he needed a 'family man' for the job. How did he put it? 'We won't be able to hire women and half the ones we've got will leave if they must worry about their superior making advances'."

Good grief. "That seems so unfair."

George shook his head, running his right thumb up and down along the top of one of his red and black striped suspenders. "But it would be wrong for me to marry." He hesitated for some time. "I'm not a regular man, and I don't think I ever shall be."

She nodded, giving him a fond smile. "I've known that since the day we visited you in the hospital."

George had barely survived poisoning. When she saw the way her Mr. Jackson had reacted to the scene, and the look George had given him in the hospital ... it had been quite touching.

He sighed. "I wish I were different. Or much older. It would make life easier. No one questions a 'confirmed bachelor'." At that, he laughed softly. "Or a spinster."

"But alas, my dear, you are **you**. You alone must decide what's best for your life."

George sat staring at the table.

Right then, Mr. Jackson and Ophelia came up. Ophelia looked at his half-eaten sandwich. "You didn't have to wait for us!"

He chuckled. "I suppose I better dig in."

Yet now, it was Ophelia's turn to fall silent, staring at her salad. What might be going on?

Mrs. Jackson turned to her Mr. Jackson sitting beside her, and took his hand under the table. "I'm so glad to be here." Not only glad to be here with him, but also with George and Ophelia, where she might be of help with their problems.

He kissed her cheek. "I'm glad you're glad, dear girl." Then he turned to the others. "After we're done here, why don't we visit the gardens?"

***

At the Grant Park gardens, Ophelia strolled arm in arm with George. "What were you talking to Pam about?"

George smiled to himself. "Oh, nothing."

"Now you got me curious."

He laughed softly to himself. "Didn't pick **you** to be the jealous type!"

"Not that." They kept strolling along, while she got her thoughts together. "It's just that ... she'll never tell me anything."

"Really?"

It was her turn to laugh. "Well, not really. I mean, if she likes or doesn't like something, then sure. But I can tell she's awful sad, and she'll never say a bit about it."

George shrugged. "She lost her first husband and her boy. Blow like that, she might never be happy."

Ophelia thought about this for a while, the gorgeous flowers around them fading from her view. "When we were come out of the bathrooms, Mr. Hector asked me if he and Pam were go away forever, if I'd follow. And I didn't know what to say!"

"Why wouldn't you?"

She had to think for a bit on that. "Well, it'd depend on where they were going. I like it here."

"They said they were going out West somewhere."

"I don't think they ever said, not to me anyway."

He was quiet for a bit. "Is that all?"

"Well, to be honest, no. This thing with the Feds after her ... it worries me." She'd never told anyone this, certainly not a man. "I love her," she whispered. "With my whole heart." She felt shaky inside, hardly able to breathe. But when she glanced at George, he simply walked along, peering at her as if truly interested in what she said. "Like a man loves a woman."

He nodded.

This made her feel better. Safe somehow. "I'd do anything for her. But ..."

"You don't know what exactly happened."

A surge of relief: he understood. "Yeah!"

Ophelia didn't know what she'd been so scared of. Georgie wasn't the kind of guy who'd laugh at you anyways, not over something serious.

They walked along a bit, then George said, "We already know most of it. She got mixed up in the Mob. When she tried to get out, they killed her husband and little boy over it." He looked out over the gardens. "It sounds like Hector and her husband were friends — he told me he made a solemn vow to keep her safe, no matter what. Even if he had to die himself." His voice shook. "The only time I've **ever** seen him scared, ever, was when he thought the Feds might find her."

He got real quiet as they walked along, then he took a deep breath. "Whatever happened, it's been over a year now. Does it really matter that much? I mean, is there anything that could've happened to her, or that she could've done, that'd make you not **love** her anymore?"

Ophelia didn't know. Mr. Hector said she didn't kill anyone. She just felt unsteady about it. "No. But I still want to know! I've told her everything. About my brother being killed in the war and the rest of my family dying from the flu." She had to stop then. "All that, and I don't even know her real name."

George nodded. They started walking again, but slower, falling behind.

She had to breathe for the rush of emotion come over her. "I grew up with a girl named Blanche. She died from the flu. But when we were together I told her everything, because I loved her. And she told me everything, too. I want that with Pam." Ophelia got out her handkerchief. "When I first met her, I promised I'd never ask what happened. Before. It was a foolish promise. And now —"

"You regret making it."

She let out a breath. "Yeah."

George gave her arm a squeeze. "Well, it's not like they're packing their bags!"

That made Ophelia laugh, in spite of how awful she felt right then.

"Let me talk to Hector, get a sense of what their plans are and where they're thinking about."

Ophelia nodded. "That sounds good."

George patted her hand. "Never you fret." He chuckled softly. "Who knows? I might be able to get some information out of the old boy."

***

As Bessie and Spot trotted beside them, Mrs. Jackson thought the roses were just as pretty this time of year as any, even though many were half in the bud. The green of the leaves was so vibrant in the afternoon sun.

She glanced back. "I wonder what those two are whispering about."

Mr. Jackson said, "How **is** our dear George?"

"His parents are pressuring him to marry."

He turned towards her, surprise and alarm upon his face. "Anyone in particular?"

"I don't think so. At least, he didn't say. But it's weighing on him. As much as he wants to be his own man, he very much wants to please his parents." A laugh burst from her unbidden. "And I doubt they ever wanted him to just be a Headwaiter, even at such a fine establishment as that one."

This made her think of her first husband. His hopes and dreams for their future were so at odds with what his parents had wanted for him. He'd found himself trapped, feeling obligated to continue in the family business, struggling against the burden of it all until the day he was murdered in it.

For the past year, the question had run through her mind every day: *what could I have done to save him?*

She rubbed the scar on the bend of her right arm. Even if she could forget that night, this reminder of it would never leave her.

"Does it still pain you?"

She shook her head. Not like that.

Mr. Jackson said, "George has some decisions to make, that's all. I just hope he can be honest about it."

Up ahead, a cluster of brightly colored parasols approached, coming the other way. With them, an old friend, some much younger couples, two small children, and one of Bessie's puppies!

Mrs. Jackson waved. "Sergeant Nestor!"

Irritation went through the older man's eyes, then he let out a laugh and tipped his cap. "Can't seem to get away from you two."

Mr. Jackson smiled to himself. The sergeant had helped hide them from their pursuers this past year. Yet they did seem to run into each other more often than either of them liked.

Sergeant Nestor turned to the men. "This is Mr. and Mrs. Jackson. Oh," he said to the children, "and Bessie, Brownie's mom."

Brownie was so big now! And well-cared for. And happy. Mrs. Jackson's eyes stung. It seemed silly to put it in that way, but her "baby" was truly in a good home.

There was a round of "nice to meet you."

The children's little eyes got wide. "Can we pet her?"

The man holding Brownie's leash said, "Let's let them greet each other, then I'll show you how to introduce yourselves."

He brought Brownie over for a bit of a family reunion. Bessie, Spot, and Brownie danced around, quite glad to see each other!

Mr. Jackson said to the rest, "This is Mr. George Neuberg and Miss Ophelia Denton."

Another round of "how do you do?"

Mrs Jackson felt quite amused. "What brings you out here today?"

"Heh," said the sergeant. "My day off."

One of the women in the back pushed a covered carriage. One of the men held a large basket. "Ah," she said. "A lovely day for a picnic."

Sergeant Nestor grinned. "So it is."

"Well, we won't keep you from your outing," said Mr. Jackson. He tipped his fedora. "A pleasure."

After some untangling of leashes, and a host of "goodbye" and "nice to meet you," the two groups parted, each going their separate ways.

Ophelia said, "Sergeant Nestor seems a nice man."

Mr. Jackson laughed, rolling his eyes. "He's nice, all right!" Then his manner sobered. "But he's been sincerely helpful to us, and I'll not forget it."

***

The couple and their friends returned to the Hotel to dress for dinner. As they entered the Myriad Hotel's expansive lobby, Mrs. Jackson saw the Myriad's Head Clerk Lee Francis and his wife Laura off to the left across the crowded lobby, waiting at the front desk.

Spot began pulling, jumping, wagging her tail ears up as they went.

"She's eager to see them," Mrs. Jackson said, but she didn't feel it. She'd grown to love little Spot, and on top of losing so much this felt like yet another loss.

Laura handed their little boy to her husband and knelt down. "Hi, Lulu!"

Mrs. Jackson said, "Lulu?"

The woman grinned. "Yep! Lee and I thought if we ever had a girl, that's what we'd call her. But we have a pretty little girl right here!" She beamed at the little dog, hugging her.

Hmm, Mrs. Jackson thought. She didn't much care for the name, but the dog was theirs now.

"Hey," Mr. Francis said. "That reminds me. Did you happen to see anything when you were up there on the roof today?"

Mrs. Jackson glanced at her Mr. Jackson; they both shook their heads, shrugging.

"Well, some of the greenhouse panes were broken. We're not sure what happened, but a couple of boys got on the elevator at the ground floor right after the man brought you," he pointed at Mr. Jackson, "claiming you'd asked them to meet you up there."

Mr. Jackson looked perplexed. "I did no such thing!"

"We saw no one," Mrs. Jackson said.

"Well," said Mr. Francis. "It was right before the man's rest break. The man who spelled him said he saw the boys go back down after you two did, but that they were well-dressed and seemed well-behaved. He never thought to ask what they were doing there."

Mrs. Jackson said, "We're most sorry that happened."

Mr. Jackson said, "We'd be happy to pay for the breakage, if you —"

"No need," Mr. Francis said. "It's been turned over to the police." He turned to his wife. "Ready to go?"

Mrs. Jackson said, "Off so soon?"

"Oh, yes," Laura said. "We're going right back home. We should let this little one get used to her new yard!"

Mrs. Jackson knelt to run her hand over the little dog's black and gold spots, feeling a pang of grief. "I'll miss you."

"Aww," Laura said warmly. "We'll have to bring her by to visit sometime."

Mrs. Jackson rose, smiling at her. "We'd like that."

But as "Lulu" left for her new home, Mrs. Jackson felt disturbed. Boys breaking the Myriad greenhouse's windows? Then blaming **them** for it?

Why would anyone do that?

3

Leaving the little family behind, George followed Hector, Pam, Bessie, and Ophie up to the suite to dress for dinner. Waiting for them were their dinner clothes, Mr. Jackson's valet Norman Vienna, and Mrs. Jackson's lady's maid, Mrs. Octavia Knight.

George considered how to approach the many things he wanted to speak with Hector about.

But after the valet brushed their dinner jackets and left, Hector turned to **him**. "My wife told me of your difficulty."

George had actually forgotten about that for the moment. "That's one way of putting it."

"I suppose you could just tell your parents you haven't found the right girl yet."

He considered it. "Now that feels like a lie. I know they'd never understand the truth. But to give them hope ...? No. It wouldn't be right."

"Well," Hector sounded surprised. "It just might take some time. I didn't think I'd be interested in **any** woman, not until my wife came along."

George laughed. "You said you liked her legs."

Hector blushed. "Yes, very much so."

"They're fine legs, I saw them on the boat last summer. That swimming outfit she wore. But ... I don't know. I just don't care for women. Not like that. They don't interest me in that way."

Hector nodded slowly. "I understand. I do. It still astonishes me that after all the years of consorting with men that I found a woman like her." He chuckled softly. "And that she's consented to have me trail behind."

George chuckled. "That one does tend to be a force of nature."

Hector grinned. "Well put."

George slumped down on the bed, dejected. "What am I going to do?"

Hector sat beside him, put his arm round his waist. "Would you like me to talk with Mr. Carlo?"

"Goodness sakes, no. I'm not even supposed to be friends with the guests, not to mention —" He felt his ears burn.

The telephone rang.

Hector stood, clapped him on the shoulder. "My apologies. It was a foolish idea." When he got to the phone, he turned back. "Perhaps try a different establishment. I'm sure someone needs a man with your ability!"

George hadn't considered it. "Yes, I think that might be a good plan."

***

While George and Mr. Jackson were being dressed by the valet, Mrs. Jackson and Ophelia were being dressed as well.

After Mrs. Knight painted their nails, Mrs. Jackson said to Ophelia, "You seem very quiet today, Pet."

She nodded. "I've got a lot on my mind."

"Anything you want to talk about?"

Ophelia glanced at Mrs. Knight.

Mrs. Knight rose. "I'll do your rinsing now, ma'am, while your nails dry." She left for the bathroom.

"Come now, Pet," said Mrs. Jackson softly, "what's troubling you?"

Ophelia hesitated for some time. Then she sighed. "Last night. I get men waiting outside the club sometimes. They want to say hello, or that they liked the show, or give me flowers. Usually, it's fun. But this one wouldn't let me pass! I had to call for the bouncers to get to the taxi."

"That sounds disturbing."

"Don't get me wrong, I wasn't hurt. But it was. Disturbing. It scared me. But the worst part was he looked plainly at my hand," she lifted up her left hand, "before he came up to me."

"I'm sorry."

"I can't help thinking: what if that's what happened to Ethel, and no one was around to help?"

"Is that what she told you?"

Ophelia hung her head. "No. But how is anyone to know? Mrs. Kilpatrick didn't even ask her side of it." She crossed her arms. "It's unfair."

"Most of what happens to women is unfair."

Ophelia snorted softly. "If I were married, I'd not be able to work there. So I suppose there's a balance."

"No one there is married? I don't understand."

Ophelia shrugged. "The ladies who do the costumes. They're married." Her head drooped, and she fell silent.

"Is that all that troubles you?"

Ophelia raised her head, her lip trembling. "Tell me who you really are."

4

How Mrs. Jackson wished she might have a peaceful, quiet life, with nothing she had to hide! But she never could. "If I do, one day someone else could ask. They might not let you pass, in a place where no one was around to help. And they could ask much less nicely."

"I don't care," said Ophelia. "I love you, that's why I want to know."

Was she sentencing Ophelia to death? "And I love **you**," she said quietly, and meant it. "That's why I don't want to put this burden upon you."

"It's not a burden," Ophelia whispered. "How can I ... how can you truly love me, yet not tell me who you really are?"

Mrs. Jackson sat there, heart heavy. Maybe if she just told her this one thing, that might be enough. She leaned forward, mindful of her still-damp nails, and whispered into Ophelia's ear.

Ophelia just sat there for a moment. "Why didn't you just **say** so?" Then she got a confused look on her face. "What do I call you?"

"Pam is fine." She took a deep breath, then let it out, feeling both contentment and loss. "If all goes well, I shall be Mrs. Pamela Jackson 'til the day I die." She smiled to herself. "There are certainly much worse things to be."

She thought that would make Ophelia laugh, but instead she peered at her with those beautiful hazel eyes, waiting for more of an answer.

"The longer I stay hidden out here," Mrs. Jackson finally said, "the longer the people who hunt me will look out here, instead of hunting the ones I love."

Ophelia grabbed her hand, instantly spoiling both their nails. "Oh, Pam. I'm sorry. I didn't mean to hurt you. Or your people. I just don't want any secrets between us."

Mrs. Jackson sighed, feeling grieved. "I don't mean to hurt you. But there are some things you don't want to know." How could she possibly put the horrors she'd been through into words, so soon? "It's better for us all if you don't know."

***

After they got their nails redone, Ophelia went with the rest to leave little Bessie with her minders over at the vet's place. A bunch of little boys, but they all seemed to be having fun.

Then Ophelia went with George, Pam and Mr. Hector to dinner at a really nice place, with candles on the tables and everything.

Pam said Mr. Hector would pay for everything, so she planned to get herself a good dinner.

But she felt unhappy.

Pam's people knew who she was. They knew everything. Why couldn't Pam just give her the truth?

Mr. Hector said to George, "Is this party going to make you very busy?"

George shrugged. "We're hiring some new waiters for the event. I'll miss it entirely." He gave an amused snort. "Busy enough downstairs with dinner service. But Mr. Carlo'll be up there to keep an eye on them."

Ophelia said, "Is that the owner?"

"Yeah," George said.

She could tell by the way he said it that George didn't like him much.

The waiter set down their drinks, took their order.

The whole while the waiter was there, Ophelia felt fidgety inside. The minute he left, she blurted out, "Where are you going?"

5

Mr. Hector's eyebrows rose. "Well," he said, "we haven't decided yet."

Ophelia glanced at George.

George said, "That's not what you told me. After whoever phoned your room."

Mr. Hector sighed. "I wanted to talk with my wife about this before I said anything."

Oops, Ophelia thought.

Mr. Hector leaned back in his chair, looked away. "My men found a place. An abandoned casino."

Pam let out a laugh.

Mr. Hector smiled at her. "I thought you'd like that. But my cousin tells me it looks a wreck. Been abandoned ten years now. It needs a proper inspection before I'd even consider it." He shrugged. "So we really **haven't** decided yet."

Ophelia sighed. "You asked if I'd go with you —"

A brief look of alarm flashed through Mr. Hector's eyes, and Ophelia realized this was something else he'd wanted to talk with Pam about. Before. "I'm sorry," Ophelia said. "I just can't answer until I know what's going on."

Pam nodded slowly, eyes going watery.

Ophelia grabbed Pam's hand. "I want to **want** to go. I really do. But —"

Pam sighed. "I understand." She looked over at Mr. Hector. "It was hardly fair to ask. So soon, before we knew we'd have to go."

Mr. Hector shook his head. "That's just it. We've been very lucky. But when we **do** have to go, it might be at a moment's notice. It could be tonight. Or it could be ten years from now. I have no idea." He leaned his elbows on the table. "That's what I suppose I was asking: if we did have to leave tonight, would you come with us?"

"Gosh." Ophelia felt fluttery inside, almost scared. "I don't know."

Pam squeezed her hand. "It's okay." But her voice sounded so very sad. "You have a life here —"

George twitched, and he got that thinking look.

"— and," Pam's eyes went to Mr. Hector, "it wasn't fair for him to ask you to make that big a move without knowing more."

Ophelia felt alarmed. "I don't want to cause a fight," she said quickly. "I'm sure he only wants what's best."

Pam gave her a warm smile. "Our fighting days are over." Then she chuckled. "Although it was ever only arguing, as much as I sometimes wanted to fight him."

George let out a surprised laugh.

"Oh, dear," Ophelia said, surprised too. "You didn't always get along!"

Mr. Hector chuckled. "No. That we didn't."

***

After dinner, the four went dancing at the Trianon. As Mr. Jackson danced with his wife, he thought about what had gone on. "You were entirely correct with what you said at dinner."

She chuckled. "And what did I get right this time?"

That made him laugh. "It wasn't fair to ask Miss Ophelia to leave with us without giving her more information."

"I wish now that you hadn't," she said sadly. "Talked to her. At least I could maintain the illusion that she'd actually come along."

This was why he hadn't wanted to bring up the matter, today of all days. "Now, you don't know one way or the other —"

"And that's the problem." Her manner became fierce. "I know what you're thinking: we can't tell them exactly where we're going! Not if there's any chance they'd not come, too. Someone might pick them up and want to know." She shook her head, then stopped in her tracks, shoulders drooping. "This is no good. They're doomed, whether they stay or go."

He took her hand. "Don't think like that."

"I can't help it. It'd be easy to learn they were close to us." Her beautiful eyes filled with tears. "I can't bear the thought of them coming to harm on my account."

He took her face in his hands and kissed her forehead as the other couples swirled round them. "They'll be well-protected, day and night. You have my word."

She smiled up at him, looking relieved. "Thank you."

He took her arm. "Let's sit for a moment."

George glanced over, but Mr. Jackson shook his head, gesturing for them to continue dancing.

The couple took seats facing the dancers around a small round table. His wife took out a cigarette, which he lit.

He needed to task some of his men to protect those two. As much as he hated to admit it, his wife was right: anyone making it this far wouldn't hesitate to get rough in order to learn what they wanted to know. And he couldn't put all his trust in the sergeant, or even Carlo.

After a few minutes, he said, "Feel better?"

"I do."

"I'm sorry I didn't speak to you about this first. But George overheard the call, and asked, and I felt excited about the prospect, and —"

She gave him a warm smile. "You didn't want to lie to him. I understand."

"Not sure I could. He's good at picking it up."

The song ended. George brought Miss Ophelia over. "Thought we'd take a breather. Mind if we join you?"

"By all means," Mr. Jackson said.

So the two pulled up chairs and sat.

"I'm going to need your help," Mr. Jackson said to no one in particular. "If this place my cousin told me about turns out to be sound, I'll need advice on what to do with it. Once I get the blueprints, that is."

George nodded, a solemn look on his face.

"Then you'll know all about it." Mr. Jackson looked at Miss Ophelia. "Fair enough?"

She nodded, not meeting his eye.

Which bothered him. She wasn't letting this go.

He hoped she wouldn't do something foolish.

After a while, George took Miss Ophelia dancing once more, and Mr. Jackson sat with his wife as she finished her cigarette.

But his mind was entirely on plans for the future.

"I've not seen you like this before," his wife said. "What's got you so intent?"

"I feel like this property could be the one. I hope so. Just think of it!"

She chuckled. "Running a casino's a lot of work. I thought you didn't much like it."

This surprised him. "What, **working**?" He shifted to lean on an elbow towards her. "I'll have you know that I built a cabin with my own hands, and helped build a cottage with my men when I was a boy. Good solid things, too." He leaned back. "I don't dislike work, but I see no reason for effort if it's not needed."

He considered it, then laughed softly to himself. "If **you** think this, I'm sure others do too!"

She laughed "As you once said, the perfect disguise! Certainly no one would expect us to be in the middle of nowhere renovating an abandoned casino."

He thought this amusing. His entire plans had been on collecting a team to do what surely needed doing.

Perhaps he didn't much like work after all! "Well, if things turn out the way I'd like, it'll be renovated long before we arrive."

***

As he danced, George caught a glimpse of Hector past the crowd.

Ophie said, "They doing okay?"

George smiled down at her. "Yeah. Talking." He craned his neck to see. "I think she's smoking."

Ophie nodded.

They continued to dance.

George liked dancing. He didn't get to do it much anymore. And Ophie was a great dancer. So this was kinda fun.

George kept thinking about what Pamela said, about already having a life here. And in the excitement of maybe going on some adventure with Hector, he'd never even thought of that.

What would his parents think, him running off? Would he be able to come home, see them again?

He'd never asked.

And somehow, he got this feeling: when Hector and Pamela Jackson left Chicago, they weren't coming back.

It made sense. If they really were running from someone — he couldn't quite believe it to be the Feds — then they couldn't come back. None of them could.

But the situation scared him. Could he do that to his parents? Just disappear?

He was their only child. They had such hopes for him. Besides, he loved them. The thought of never seeing them again hurt.

"What's wrong?"

Ophie's voice startled him. Heart pounding, he said, "Just thinking too much."

She giggled.

Hector had been right. If they needed to go, they might not have any notice.

George knew he had to figure this out, and soon.

5

If George couldn't move ahead at the Hotel, he needed a better plan. And one thing George knew he could do was sport. So the next day before work, he went to the fitness club Hector had introduced him to.

George had gotten his own membership, and now went there more often than Hector did. So he'd gotten to know the people there, particularly the owner.

Fortunately for him, Mr. Abney was at the desk, taking towels out of a crate, fluffing and refolding them. He glanced up. "Well, hello there, Neuberg! Don't often see you here this early! What'll it be today?"

"I was wondering if you needed a front manager," George said.

The man's face turned guarded. "Really?"

"Yes, sir."

He seemed even more uneasy. "What made you want to change your position? I thought you just started as Headwaiter last summer."

George shrugged. "I like it there fine. But it looks as if I'm not going anywhere with the company."

He glanced away. "I'm not hiring."

"Are you certain? I mean, look at you. You're the owner, and your business does exceptionally well." A laugh burst from him. "Surely you could hire someone to fluff the towels!"

Mr. Abney set the towel on the counter. "How old are you, son?"

"Twenty-seven."

"Spend time in the war?"

"No, sir. I mean, I never saw combat. My family builds boats, so my father got an exemption so I might work the shipyards. I have design experience, but it was mostly machinery work."

"So you served beside many women, I take it."

George nodded.

"So why haven't you settled down, then, hmm?"

George hated lying to the man. "Just haven't found the right girl, that's all."

Mr. Abney scoffed. "This is a men's club, son. Quality gentlemen come here —"

George began to feel desperate. "Wait —"

The older man held up his hand. "I'm not casting any aspersions on your character. I myself didn't marry until I was almost thirty!"

He reached over to put a hand on George's shoulder. "I don't think there's a thing wrong with you." He took a deep breath. "But as someone who's been in your shoes, I have to tell you straight: these folks will. And the older you get, the more they'll talk. You're a good-looking, fit man, with steady finances, surrounded by a sea of unmarried women. They'll wonder why you won't marry. Are you shell-shocked? Immoral? A bootlegger? Or," his voice went to a whisper, "of an unsuitable temperament to be round unclothed men."

George was so stunned he couldn't speak.

He took his hand off of George's shoulder. "I'm sorry to have shocked you with such language, sir, truly I am. I don't believe this of you for one minute. Why, if I did, I'd tell you to find work in Towertown."

"What's that?"

"Heh," Mr. Abney said. "You don't want to know." He sighed, glancing away. "I like you. You have a good job and a fine reputation. I want you to succeed. If you were married, you're right: I **could** use a hand here." He peered at him. "You want to move ahead. I understand. We all do. But you have your whole life ahead of you." He gave a nod, with a look that made George think of an owl. "Slow down, son. First things first."

George stumbled down the steps, hurt, deeply embarrassed, angry.

Now he understood his father's concern at him refusing to marry. His mother's worry, her tears.

Was he destined to forever be in a dead-end job? Even if he took over his father's business, would there be people refusing to buy his yachts, looking at him with suspicion — merely because he hadn't **married**?

Things couldn't go on like this.

6

A week later, Mr. and Mrs. Jackson (and Bessie) stepped out of the elevator onto the Myriad Hotel's rooftop. Jazz music hung in the air. Before them stood a thin black metal railing with electric lights strung atop, and a sign in a black holder with a large arrow pointing to the right: GALA.

The railing guided them to the right, around the elevator shaft and past the exit door to the stair. Brass stanchions stood on either side, and a fat velvety-black rope with brass on both ends blocked their path.

The metal railing had been placed all the way to the concrete banisters on both ends of the rooftop, separating Monsieur's kitchen gardens from the party before them.

And what a scene it was!

To the left, torches, candles, and electric lights lit the area almost as well as day might. A huge buffet had been spread along the rail, and a dozen people mingled in front of the grand greenhouse. Someone had moved an upright piano to the roof, and a jazz quintet in the far left corner closest to the gardens explained the music.

To the right, the pool was dark, only lit slightly by the far reaches of the dazzling display and the fat votives placed on the pavement around its edge.

The night was clear and warm with no moon. Stars twinkled overhead.

Mrs. Jackson said, "A perfect night for a party."

Mr. Jackson chuckled softly.

She felt weary. They'd been awakened by a telephone call in the midst of night. And even though her Mr. Jackson had gotten up to answer, she felt as though she'd missed some sleep.

Mr. Jackson hadn't mentioned the call the next morning, and she'd forgotten about it until now. What might it have been about?

Mr. Montgomery Carlo came hurrying up to unhook the rope. "Welcome! Right this way." A big, swarthy man with hooded dark eyes, Mr. Carlo was the owner of the Myriad Hotel.

Mrs. Jackson felt touched that he would personally show them such kindness. Although they **were** in the Myriad's best suite. And Mr. Jackson was known to be a fabulous tipper.

Mr. Carlo led them over to a woman wearing a fine mink stole, a beautiful set of large pearls, silver-rimmed spectacles, and a blue silk dress overlaid in lace. She was at least seventy, with silver-gold hair and bright blue eyes. She'd been speaking with a dark-haired man barely out of his teens until Mr. Carlo tapped her shoulder. "Mrs. Lydia Von Bilten, Mr. Charles De Rege, may I present Hector and Pamela Jackson."

The young man rolled his eyes.

"Oh!" Mrs. Jackson said, taking the old woman's lace-gloved hand. "I'm so glad to meet you! I read about your garden club in the paper."

Mrs. Von Bilten smiled at her, but the smile didn't reach her eyes. "A pleasure."

Mr. Jackson had reached out his hand as well, but apparently the woman didn't take notice.

Mr. Carlo gave them a glance. "This is Mr. Hector Jackson, one of our hosts."

The woman nodded to him. "Good to meet you."

Still she didn't take his hand, so Mr. Jackson tipped his fedora. "A pleasure."

Mr. Carlo seemed put out. "We'll let you return to your —"

Mrs. Von Bilten turned away.

A tall, brown-haired waiter who was perhaps twenty passed by. The tag on the man's chest read: Hugh.

Young Charles snapped his fingers at the man. "You there! Another drink."

Mr. Carlo said to Mr. Jackson, "I'm dreadfully sorry. Come, let's see what Monsieur has prepared for us."

Monsieur, of course, was the Hotel's Chef. He wasn't at the affair, being over thirty flights below running dinner service with George. But one of the waiters he'd hired, a short blond fellow with spectacles, stood ready to replenish the table. His name-tag read: Russell.

And the table was well-stocked. Canapés of all sorts, cubed meats, sliced cheeses, diced fruit speared upon toothpicks. An array of cut vegetables alongside sauces galore. Olives, nuts, bacon-wrapped figs.

Mrs. Jackson looked back: instead of surveying the table, Mr. Jackson stood watching the brown-haired waiter as he moved about the room. She went on tiptoe to speak in his ear. "He **is** nice, isn't he?"

Mr. Jackson let out an embarrassed laugh, blushing. "I suppose."

She took his hand. She knew he fancied men, but it wasn't like him to be so obvious about it. "Let's get you some dinner, shall we?"

Russell had been slicing cheese into cubes with a rather large knife. He dipped the knife in water and wiped it perfectly clean.

Mr. Carlo had been sampling several of the bacon-wrapped figs.

Neither had noticed a thing.

A very pale red-haired waiter who wore his hair short in the back with long bangs parted in the middle stood at the end of the buffet, carefully pouring flutes of champagne. His name-tag read: Victor.

Young Victor's hand shook slightly as he poured. Cases of bottles rose to his waist beside him.

Mr. Jackson chuckled. "I see now why the sergeant isn't here."

Mr. Carlo laughed. "What the police don't know won't hurt them."

Mr. Jackson glanced in the direction of the brown-haired waiter and sighed. "I suppose I **should** eat something." He picked up a porcelain saucer and began filling it.

Not wanting to look at the champagne, Mrs. Jackson gazed out across the rooftop. Two black wire tables large enough for six and matching chairs had been placed on either side of the greenhouse entryway.

Past the greenhouse, a thin man in his middle forties with straight black hair parted in the center and a waxed mustache leaned against the banister smoking a cigarette from a long thin holder as he flirted with a blonde half his age.

The man wore black gloves and a black coat, embroidered in purples and reds, which reached to the floor around his forest green shirt and trousers.

The blonde's sleeveless dress was sequined in red, dipped low in front, and to Mrs. Jackson's surprise, showed the woman's legs almost up to her knee! A matching headband across her forehead and bright Cupid's bow lips.

Perhaps sensing Mrs. Jackson's gaze, the woman turned her head, giving a bright smile and a wave.

"Ah." A young woman's wry voice came from behind. "You've seen our Bohemian."

Mrs. Jackson turned to face her.

About the same age as the waiters, this woman held a half-full champagne flute in her left hand. She wore a fine, richly beaded dark brown dress reaching to her mid-calf with lacy quarter length sleeves and a matching headband over curly brown hair. The young woman held out her right hand as Bessie sniffed at her shoes. "Ruby Carlisle."

Mrs. Jackson took Ruby's hand. The woman had a dark brown mole on her left lower cheek, just above the level of her mouth. Real, not painted. Quite fashionable.

"A pleasure." She let go, looked around. "What brings you here?"

"I could say the same. We're a family of sorts. My father was a greenhouse architect for many years."

"I see."

Ruby gestured with her chin at the Bohemian. "He builds greenhouses too. Although I wonder why he bothered to show up. He hates Horace."

"Really."

Ruby laughed. "They all hate each other. But it's best to be seen. You never know when some event will bring your next client."

Mrs. Jackson said, "You're so knowledgeable. Are you a designer as well?"

"Here? I'm a woman. I might be able to find work in Paris, or perhaps Milan. But this is an old boy's club, always has been." She shrugged, then downed her drink. "I have no interest in it. My sister, perhaps."

The brown-haired waiter passed with an empty tray. Ruby set the glass upon it. "Get me another."

His answer was too low for Mrs. Jackson to hear, but from their body language, the young man had said something rude and insulting.

Ruby rolled her eyes and let out a sigh.

Definitely not the usual for waiters at the Myriad Hotel. "Is your sister here?"

Ruby gave a one-shoulder shrug, glancing away. "You'll meet her soon enough."

At that, Ruby drifted off without saying goodbye.

Mr. Jackson came up with a saucer full of hors d'oeuvres. He handed Mrs. Jackson a glass of water. "Who was that?"

"Her father used to build greenhouses. I guess most all of them do."

"Interesting," Mr. Jackson said, then popped a grape into his mouth.

Mrs. Jackson took a drink of her water. It was tepid, but she was thirsty.

"There's a reporter here," Mr. Jackson said. "And a photographer. Apparently some actress is expected."

A gruff male voice broke in. "There's always one of them at these sorts of things."

Mrs. Jackson turned to face the man.

At least sixty. Short, wide, graying, holding a well-worn brown leather briefcase, smelling of pipe tobacco. With a tweed overcoat and brass spectacles, he seemed somewhat underdressed for the affair.

She held out her hand. "Pamela Jackson. And this is my husband, Hector."

The man tipped his cap. "A pleasure."

Mrs. Jackson said, "Are you a greenhouse designer?"

"Heh," the man said dismissively. "Wouldn't catch me dead in one of those things, not in this city."

Mr. Jackson laughed. "So what brings you here?"

"I'm supposed to meet someone." He sighed, taking out a pocketwatch on its chain and peering at it. "Late, as usual." Replacing the watch, he retrieved a well-worn pipe from his overcoat's pocket, set the briefcase between his feet, and lit the pipe.

Mr. Carlo, a man holding a notepad, and a man holding a camera all rushed past.

Mrs. Jackson turned towards the commotion.

A willowy woman in her late thirties with straight brown hair cut in a bob and bright red lipstick stood at the velvety rope, accompanied by a tall, muscular man. Both wore black; the woman's sleeveless dress was beaded down to the fringe covering her mid-calf. Her beaded headband had several raven's feathers at the back arrayed as a fan.

"The actress," the old man said, as if it were obvious.

The reactions of the rest were interesting. The Bohemian didn't stir, although the blonde pulled at him, urging him to. Finally, the young woman abandoned him to dash across the rooftop towards the pair, heels clattering. The old woman gave a glance over her shoulder, then returned to her conversation. Ruby looked bored, the waiters awestruck.

Mr. Carlo waved off the onlookers, escorting the actress and her companion — the man looked like a bodyguard more than anything else — to the buffet.

And as yet, there'd been no sign of the architect. Where was he?

7

Right then, George Neuberg was in the dining room of the Myriad, overseeing the dinner service. Directing the waiters, taking reservations, escorting the more important guests to their tables. It was all routine by now, even to the matrons who inevitably complained about something.

Will was doing quite well — going table to table promoting the evening's special, shaking the hands of the more important guests, checking on the waiters.

A silver-haired woman in a tan beaded dinner gown came up to his podium, a small golden poodle in her arms. "Oh, Mr. Neuberg! I'm so happy to see you!"

"Why, Duchess Cordelia! It's always a pleasure." He offered his arm, which she took. "Right this way."

He escorted the woman to her table and held the chair for her. As she sat, Floyd came up with a small porcelain bowl of chopped meat, setting it on the floor beside her — for her dog.

"Simply marvelous," said the Duchess to them both, setting little Bertie on the floor. "Thank you ever so much."

George smiled at her. "You're **most** welcome." Duchess Cordelia Stayman was one of the good ones. She never made a fuss, even though she was related to

Mr. Carlo somehow. The woman really seemed to care about people's welfare. And she invited the staff to her rooms for dominoes every Tuesday.

Pity about her husband.

Thinking about Albert Stayman reminded George of his father, and as he returned to the host station, he wondered what he possibly could do to solve the dilemma he found himself in.

He liked this job. It suited him. But if he were to travel with Hector and Pamela, he needed to earn more. And every interview he'd had brought up his unmarried status.

It felt so frustrating!

Another couple came up, and he checked their reservation. Not guests of the Hotel, so he waved Floyd up, passing the couple off to him.

And then there was the issue of Hector and Pam leaving. He didn't know if he could bear never seeing Hector again. But abandoning his parents without even saying goodbye seemed unthinkable.

What should he do?

The telephone rang. "Yes, sir. I have a spot open for 8:45." He made a note in the schedule. "You're quite welcome, sir."

A hand fell on his shoulder. Replacing the receiver, he turned towards whoever this might be.

Will stood there. "Is all well?"

George blinked. "I suppose. Why?"

"You don't seem yourself tonight."

George shrugged. "Got a lot on my mind."

Will chuckled. "Don't we all. Listen, 24 wants to pay his tab tomorrow. I told him we don't do that unless they're Hotel guests."

"Heh." George felt amused. "I'll handle it. Come on, you'll learn something."

As they went to table 24, George thought: *is this what being a father feels like?* He wasn't sure, but as he privately informed the gentleman that he could either pay his bill or the police would be notified, he felt pride at the awe in the younger man's eyes.

The older gentleman hemmed and hawed, and red-faced, got the money from his table. "Thank you kindly, sir," George said. "Come again."

Dad's just trying to steer me the right way, George thought. *He loves me.*

But in his situation, George didn't know what the right way was.

***

The rooftop was warm, the day's heat radiating from below. Mrs. Jackson enjoyed the chance to sit, listen to the musicians.

Normally at an event like this, her Mr. Jackson would be chatting with everyone. Instead, he'd spent the entire evening either on the phone or jotting on a notepad he'd hidden away in his tuxedo.

She looked over at him as they sat together. "You're awfully quiet."

He smiled warmly. "Just pondering my next move."

"Wait. Did you hear back already?"

He beamed. "I did."

"So **that** was the mysterious midnight call!"

He chuckled. "My cousin had spent three days going over the place. It's two hours to the nearest telephone, and he was in such a hurry to report back that he forgot the time. But the news is good. The foundation and weight-bearing beams are perfectly sound. It'll need a new roof, and plumbing, and updated electrical —"

"But we're putting in an offer."

He nodded.

Mrs. Jackson threw her arms round him, right there in front of everyone. "Oh, I'm so pleased." Tears of relief sprung to her eyes: they had someplace to go.

Mr. Jackson patted her back, then hugged her, kissing her hair. "You see? It'll all work out."

She pulled back, fetching her handkerchief so as not to ruin her makeup. "But what if they don't accept the offer? What if —?"

"Now hush. Flan is **very** good at negotiation." He laughed softly to himself. "Even better than I. Now stop fretting and try to enjoy the party!"

The door to the stairs opened. A man perhaps her age entered the rooftop and called out, "He's coming!"

A few moments later, a pale, dark-haired, overweight man in his late fifties staggered onto the scene through the door to the stairs, accompanied by two men wearing the livery of the Hotel. He mopped his brow with a handkerchief, panting.

Mr. Carlo strolled over, holding out his hand. The man shook it, then fanned out his tuxedo, which even from here seemed damp with sweat. The two bellhops tipped their hats to Mr. Carlo then disappeared around the corner with the other man, presumably to take the elevator down.

Mr. Jackson sounded incredulous. "He climbed thirty-three **floors**?"

Mrs. Von Bilten, her insolent young companion, and the rest began moving towards the man. "Thirty-four, actually," Charles said dryly as he passed.

The old man moved fastest, pushing past the others to get to the architect.

Mrs. Jackson said, "Perhaps the man's afraid of elevators. Many are."

"Good grief," Mr. Jackson said. "That's dedication!"

This made Mrs. Jackson take pause. Why would a man climb thirty-three flights just to attend a party? The party **was** in his honor, but ... "It's not like you to hold back on such good news."

The old man seemed angry, gesturing at him. The architect said something to the older man which seemed to mollify him.

Mr. Jackson chuckled. "Just an oversight, my dear. It was rather late, and I'd given the matter over to Flan. So by the morning, it'd gone completely from my mind." He gave her a fond smile. "I promised never to lie to you, and I try always to keep my promises."

She felt abashed. "Well, yes, of course." Taking a deep breath, she rose. He rose also, and she took his arm. "Why don't we meet our guest of honor?"

For such it had to be: even the Bohemian had deigned to saunter over to the architect, wearing a wry, derisive smile as he offered his hand.

Mr. Horace Rothmore had dark blue eyes. His face was pale, and he had a nervous way about him. Even so, she liked him. He reminded her of someone.

Mr. Jackson offered his hand. "Hector Jackson at your service, sir."

Mr. Carlo, who'd hovered nearby, said, "This is one of our hosts for this evening."

Mr. Rothmore had already grasped Mr. Jackson's hand. "Good to meet you, sir."

Mr. Jackson turned to her and said, "May I present my wife Pamela."

The architect beamed. "And what a lovely woman she is, too!" He grasped her hand in both of his.

A bit sweaty, but she appreciated the gesture. "Thank you, sir."

Mr. Carlo said, "Would you care to sample the buffet? We also have a fine array of refreshments, if you wish to indulge."

He perked up. "I would indeed!"

Mr. Carlo and the architect moved off.

Mrs. Jackson said to Mr. Jackson, "What's this about being the host?"

A short, wry laugh burst from him. "Since I've done service for Mr. Carlo, he's refusing to take the entirety of our bills. Since I refused to stay unless he did, he's put a portion towards the hosting of these affairs." He shrugged. "A perfectly reasonable arrangement."

The man's appearance, his smile, his manner, the way he moved ... "He reminds me a bit of —"

Mr. Jackson nodded. "Yes. I see it now."

Grief pinched her face, her chest. "If he would've lived." Her eyes stung. "He of all people deserved to live." *If only I'd died instead,* she thought. Her beloved could've lived out his days with their son. "Maybe I should go back. Let them kill me too."

Mr. Jackson's embrace was quick, warm and gentle. "My dear girl. This is all nonsense. What good would dying do? You did the best you possibly could!" He gently grasped her upper arms, drew her away, his dark eyes peering into hers. "Why torture yourself so?"

He'd never said this before, and it surprised her. "I don't know. It's so unfair for you to be chased out into the wilderness, when you've done nothing wrong."

He smiled to himself. "I chose to follow you." He took her chin, gazed into her eyes. "They could chase us over the entire world, and it wouldn't matter. I'll keep you safe and well, to the end of our days." He stroked the side of her cheek. "I promise."

Mr. Carlo called out, "Mr. Horace Rothmore will give us a tour of his greenhouse in twenty minutes!"

Pleased murmurings all round.

"This should be interesting," said Mr. Jackson. "I've not yet been inside."

8

Mr. Rothmore looked chagrined when the strange old man refused to enter with them.

Mr. Jackson thought that the greenhouse was everything one might expect: vaulted glass ceiling, lush foliage, spongy earthen paths. The place reminded him of his wife's request for a garden at their new home.

The sound of water came from the other side of the greenhouse. Out West was often dry, and in places, barren. How might he have a garden like this created for her there?

Mr. Rothmore had been speaking as they walked. "The upper panels are on a mechanical timer set to the sun's passage during the spring through the fall, to open in the afternoon for proper ventilation. Also, there are controls to adjust for temperature and humidity, as well as shade covers which deploy automatically. This is all to ensure the plants are kept at their finest."

This seemed a remarkable plan. He made a mental note to approach the architect at some later date about a custom design for their property — whichever one they ended up acquiring.

But he hoped the owners accepted his offer. The place intrigued him. Why spend so much time and money to set up a casino — which sounded like a sure bet out there with the cowboys and gamblers — then abandon it?

He laughed softly to himself. It didn't matter. All that mattered was that the building was sound, and barring any unforeseen circumstances, would soon be theirs.

The young woman his wife had been speaking with earlier stood nearby, seemingly put off by his laughter. "What's so funny?"

He shrugged. "Just thought of something amusing."

An older man with an impressive moustache and a floor-length embroidered jacket turned to the young woman. "My dear Oyster, not everything is about you."

She flushed red, scowling.

This made him laugh. "Oyster?"

The man gave him a strange look. "A personal joke, I suppose." Then he seemed amused. "The way she clams up when you ask her anything."

The young woman shook herself, rolling her eyes.

The group had made their way to the fountain, a mini-waterfall reaching almost to the roof. Beside it, a large stack of wide bags labeled, "Decorative Stone" reached almost head-high. Some crates of tools, two ladders, and the unassembled bits of much smaller black wire tables and chairs lay neatly stacked beyond that.

Pointing to the area in front of the waterfall, Mr. Carlo said, "We're putting in a small patio for our guests to enjoy."

The burly man beside Mr. Carlo said, "That pile looks a bit high. Isn't that dangerous?"

Mr. Carlo shrugged, patting a bag of stone. The stack didn't budge. "It'd take a strong man to topple that."

The rest laughed.

They moved on, around the greenhouse. The views were lovely, and the air was pleasantly warm. Even so, it seemed a bit close in there, and Mr. Jackson felt glad to exit into the fresh night breeze.

***

An hour later, Mrs. Jackson looked around and let out a weary sigh. There had been toasts, and dancing, but she didn't feel much like either.

The younger folks — including the waiters —were drinking heavily, chasing after and teasing each other. The older ones alternated between ignoring and sniping at each other. The actress and her bodyguard were nowhere to be seen.

The jazz quintet played dutifully. Even though she applauded them at their breaks, to the rest they seemed in a different world, completely unnoticed by the crowd.

All this time, Mr. Jackson had been scribbling on his notepad, as intent on his work as if he'd been downstairs in their suite, rather than at an event.

The old man paced about, unlit pipe in one hand and briefcase in another. Finally he went to the architect, shaking his pipe angrily. The architect spoke sharply, then pointed towards the greenhouse and went inside.

The exchange seemed to mollify the old man. He approached their table. "Mind if I join you?"

Her Mr. Jackson glanced up with a startled expression. "Of course! Please do."

The old man pulled up a chair, looking disgruntled.

Mrs. Jackson said, "I hope all is well?"

The old man said, "I told my driver it'd take ten minutes. It's been two hours!" He crossed his arms, a scowl on his face.

Bessie went to the man and put her paws on his leg.

The man's scowl faded. He patted Bessie's head. "Pretty little thing you've got there."

"This is Bessie," Mrs. Jackson said.

"Well, hello, Bessie."

Bessie wagged her fluffy black tail, ears up.

"Come on, girl," Mrs. Jackson said. "Let's get you something to eat." They went to the buffet, where she picked out two saucers of food, one for her, the other for Bessie, and returned to the table.

From over by the pool came an outraged shriek and a huge splash.

Mrs. Jackson sat, putting Bessie's saucer on the ground beside her. "I wonder what that's all about."

Several minutes later, Ruby came storming across the rooftop towards Mr. Carlo, hair and clothing drenched, makeup streaming down. "Your waiter pushed me into the pool!"

Gasps came from all sides.

Mr. Carlo scowled, pointing towards the brown-haired waiter. "You there! Get over here this minute!"

Hugh came past their table, yelling, "It's a lie! She —"

Ruby yelled, "You ruined my dress!"

"That's not true!" He pointed back at the pool. "She ran past me and jumped in! I —"

"You're fired," said Mr. Carlo. "And you'll be getting no reference from me."

"This is unfair!" Throwing up his hands, Hugh rushed towards the pool.

Mr. Carlo watched him go, then seeing no further upset, turned to Ruby. "I'll have your dress replaced, miss, no charge."

Ruby didn't look mollified. "It's one of a kind, custom-made."

Mr. Carlo handed over a card. "Just contact my manager with the details. We'll have another one made up for you right away." He snapped his fingers at Victor. "Get this young lady a towel."

Victor turned even paler than he already was. "R-right away, sir." The young red-haired waiter returned with a rather large golden towel edged in cobalt. Hands shaking, he draped the towel over the shivering girl's shoulders, covering her to her knees.

"Heh," the old man said. "Most interesting thing that's happened all night."

Mrs. Jackson glanced around. The food, after having sat on the buffet all this time, was nothing special. She finished her glass of water. "I wonder where our guest of honor's gone to?"

The old man snorted. "Probably saw some plant that needed tending." He heaved himself up, then grabbed his briefcase. "I'll go fetch him."

Mrs. Jackson rose. "Might I join you?"

Mr. Jackson scrambled to his feet. "My apologies! I completely —"

"Pay it no mind," Mrs. Jackson said, feeling amused. "This gentleman and I are going in search of our architect."

But her Mr. Jackson' eyes were back on his notepad. "Very well, dear. I'll await your return."

Mrs. Jackson chuckled as she and the older man went along. "This is so unlike him! He's usually the life of the party." She peered down at her little dog trotting beside them. "Isn't that right, Bessie?"

The old man laughed, then held the greenhouse door open for her. "A man who does business at a party is my kind of guy."

The inside of the greenhouse was humid, well-lit, and utterly silent. Mrs. Jackson called out, "Mr. Rothmore? Are you in here?"

Bessie whined, pulling on her leash.

Mrs. Jackson followed. "It seems like she smells something."

Bessie led them past lush plants, towards the waterfall. The water no longer flowed.

Near the ground, beside the drying stone structure, a panel lay open. Next to that, a pair of men's shoes pointed down, attached to two legs covered by two large bags of decorative rock.

They'd found the architect.

7

As it was somewhat hidden by a large plant, Mrs. Jackson hadn't noticed the stained glass door on the other side of the waterfall until then.

She might not have noticed it at all, but it opened.

The old man's eyes were searching the ground. "Do you see a briefcase anywhere? It'd be just like mine."

Mrs. Jackson shook her head. "No."

The brown-haired waiter stuck his head in. "I went round to see where she'd come from and I found the door ajar." His eyes went to the architect and he gasped.

"Call for the police," the old man said. "There's been an accident."

The young man disappeared, his running footsteps heading towards the phone stand by the pool.

A gurgling sound came from underneath the bag.

The old man said, "Good gravy! Could he possibly have survived?"

"Help!" Mrs. Jackson cried out.

The old man retreated, eyes wide. "I have a bad back. I'm not allowed to lift anything heavier than my briefcase, by doctor's orders. Certainly not something like that!"

She tried pulling on the bag. It shifted, just a little. But a moan came from the man.

Was she hurting him? This bag needed to be lifted, and she knew she wasn't strong enough to do it alone. "Go, then. Hurry. Get help!"

***

George was just getting the 8:45 crowd seated when the front desk clerk came rushing up. "A Mrs. Kilpatrick is here to see you."

George felt confused. "Did she say what it's about?"

"No, sir, she just said it was urgent."

Will stood off to one side, at a table full of guests. George got Will's attention. "I need you to take the reins for a minute."

"Sure, boss," Will said cheerfully.

"I'll be right back." George followed the clerk through the frosted glass double doors to the lobby.

Mrs. Kilpatrick stood at the front desk, her apron still on, holding a handkerchief. When she saw him, she visibly relaxed. "Oh, dear goodness, they found you! I tried calling but they said you were busy, so I —"

George held up a hand. "What happened?"

"It's Miss Ophelia. The Patruni club called. She never arrived —"

Terror hit. Something happened to Ophie? All sorts of horrible scenarios began going through his mind.

"— but I don't understand it. She left **early**! She told the other girls she was going to the library first. Why would she go **there**? Do you know what's going on?"

George took a deep breath, heart racing. He had to think. "We'll need a taxi —"

The night clerk nodded. "Right away, sir."

He put his hand on the older woman's shoulder, feeling shaky. "You did the right thing." He felt like he couldn't breathe right. "I'll take you home in case she calls there." He took a deep breath, trying to calm down. This lady was counting on him. "Then I'll go look for her myself."

8

Mrs. Jackson crouched, tears streaming down her face, as the gurgling noises from the architect slowed. She'd liked the man, and now he was gravely hurt, maybe even dying.

Settle yourself, she thought. It'd simply been an accident, nothing more.

Soon the greenhouse was filled with people running towards her, Bessie barking, women sobbing, men shouting. The old lady had her hands to her face, wailing, "Noooo! Noooo!" at the top of her lungs.

Mr. Jackson rushed to Mrs. Jackson. "Are you hurt?"

"No," said Mrs. Jackson. "But he was making a noise. He might still be alive! Help me get these off him."

At once, Mr. Jackson went round to grasp a corner of the bag.

Mrs. Von Bilten, whose mink stole was now nowhere to be seen, clasped her hands in front of herself, as if she might be praying. "Oh, please let him be alive!" Then she shouted at the rest, "Well? Do something!"

Mr. Jackson and the Bohemian lifted the bags off Mr. Rothmore and placed them to the side.

But Mr. Rothmore lay unmoving.

Mrs. Jackson felt for a pulse and could find none. She looked up at the rest and shook her head.

The old lady began sobbing. Charles comforted her.

Mr. Carlo was aghast. "How could this possibly have happened?"

The Bohemian said, "I don't see how this was natural. The stack hasn't toppled. It's like ... like the bags were **dropped** upon him."

Mr. Jackson pointed. The two ladders that had been stacked together by the disassembled chairs and tables were now leaned upon the steel supports on each side of the stack. "Two people did this. Or one exceedingly strong man."

All eyes went to the burly man and the actress standing to his left.

The man took a step back, eyes wide, hands to his chest. "Surely you can't think **I** would do this? Why would I want this guy dead? We'd only just met!"

The woman placed her left hand on his, and a glittering large ring lay there. "He can't have done it," she said to them all. "He was with me until we heard the shouting."

The little blonde next to the Bohemian giggled. "I was coming from the toilet and saw them kissing!"

The actress blushed. "He just proposed."

"Oooh," the blonde said. "I love your ring."

"Enough!" The old man sounded outraged. "A man is **dead**! And my **property** has been stolen!"

Mr. Jackson said, "What property?"

"That's none of your concern." He looked around, scowling. "Where's that waiter gotten to?" He pointed towards the back door. "I told him to phone the police!"

Mr. Carlo's face turned horrified. "He was **in** here?"

"After we found the body," said Mrs. Jackson. "He seemed as surprised as we were." But she felt curious. "Do you know what that panel here is for?"

"Electrical," the old man said gruffly. "The water turns off when the panel's opened."

Mrs. Jackson moved gingerly around the dead man to peer into the panel. The space was just large enough to fit a briefcase similar to the one the old man held.

She glanced back at the old man. "What was it he came for?"

The old man ignored her, still searching the ground around him.

Ruby peered at the scene from behind the rest. Her hair was wet, and she still wore the towel. But her makeup was perfect.

Bessie pulled at her leash, away from the quieted waterfall, past the dead man, and past the piles of unassembled table and chair.

"Look here," the Bohemian said. "At the marks on the ground." He stared back at them, face astonished. "It looks like he was dragged!"

***

At any other time, George would've found Mrs. Kilpatrick incredibly annoying. But she'd evidently thought about the events of the day.

"Miss Ethel called, asking for Miss Ophelia." The woman's hand went to her mouth. "Oh. I shouldn't be telling you this."

"No," George said. "It's fine. She already told me what happened."

"Well," Mrs. Kilpatrick said, embarrassed, "The girl called, after I told her not to. I almost didn't want to let her take the call, but that dear little Ophelia's been downcast ever since Ethel left."

George glanced outside the cab: no sign of Ophelia anywhere. "Do you know what the call was about?"

"No ... they whispered for some time." She puffed up, suddenly offended. "I don't have two lines, sir, for me to listen in on private conversations. They may be young. But these are grown women, and will I treat them as such."

"No offense, meant, ma'am: I only wondered if maybe they were to meet somewhere."

The woman looked rattled. "I never considered it!" She bit her lower lip. "I don't think so. Miss Ophelia just happened to mention to Zinnie that she'd go to the library before work, or I'd never have known."

After George dropped Mrs. Kilpatrick at her home — with strict instructions to keep the girls off the line in case Ophie might call — he had the taxi take the route someone might walk to the library.

The whole time, he peered out of the window, heart in his throat.

If she wasn't at the library, he didn't know what he was going to do. Where could Ophie have gone? Had someting happened to her? He couldn't think of any other reason for her not to arrive at work.

"What's she look like?"

George turned to the man, startled. "I —"

The taxi driver chuckled. "Never seen a man get so worked up about anything other than his gal."

*His **gal**?* He and Ophie were friends, sure. If he had his way, they'd go dancing together every night. But she'd never wanted anything else, which suited him just fine. "Short, reddish blonde curls, dark mustard-colored hat and coat."

"Sounds sweet," the man said. "Sure hope you find her. You getting married?"

George felt just a little annoyed. "No ..."

"No offense. Just ... you might want to grab this one before she gets away. If you take my meaning."

George flopped back in the seat, mind reeling. His heart thudded in his chest. He'd never conceived of such a thing. "Just get us there, will you?" He had to find her. He couldn't bear the thought of never seeing her again.

***

Meanwhile, the group in the greenhouse peered at the ground. Definite drag marks, scratched into the soft mossy walkway, with dribbles of what looked like water along the way. Following these led to the front corner of the glass structure.

Mrs. Jackson smelled an acrid, metallic odor. Much of the ground was dark. Water had been splashed upon the area, but spatters of blood lay upon the foliage. "Where did this blood come from?"

Those assembled there looked at the dead man, still face-down on the ground, then rushed to his side.

"We should take pictures of how we found him," the Bohemian said, "for the police."

The photographer, who'd not moved from staring at the dead man, jerked as if startled.

Charles De Rege said, "Isn't it a bit late for that?"

Mr. Jackson said, "It's a fine idea." He turned to the photographer. "Go on, sir."

The photographer looked as if he might be sick. But he took several photos of the area.

"I don't see much blood here beside him," said Mrs. Jackson. "I wonder where it came from?"

The old man growled. "Let's have a look."

Amidst protests of "No!" and "We should wait for the police!" and "We shouldn't move the body!" he pushed past and turned the architect over.

Mr. Horace Rothmore's throat had been cut.

9

The actress fainted, her gentleman only barely catching her. Mrs. Von Bilten screamed, sobbing, and dashed out. The little blonde said, "I better make sure she's okay." and followed her.

The burly man moved his fiancée to the side, leaned her onto a small tree and fanned her with his fedora. The old man surveyed the scene, scoffed, and left through the back door. Young Miss "Oyster" hurried to follow him.

Astonished, Mr. Jackson murmured to himself, "This is a murder!"

The camera flashed as the photographer took a picture of the dead man.

Charles De Rege drawled, "You **really** think so. And what **other** brilliant ideas do you have?"

Mr. Jackson, to his credit, ignored the young man. He took his wife's hand. "Let's find that waiter."

The two went out of the back door into relative darkness, lit only by the inner glow of the greenhouse. When they reached the telephone cabana, the older man and Miss "Oyster" stared at the pieces of wrapped electrical cord in their hands.

The young woman looked up at him, fear in her eyes, and spoke too loudly. "The phone wires were cut!"

Startled murmurs as the others heard. Several came over to investigate.

Who would cut the phone wires, when they had a dead man —?

He felt horrified. "The murderer's here with us!"

Only the killer wouldn't want the police notified. Only the killer wouldn't want the architect to get help.

And the young brown-haired waiter was nowhere to be seen.

He'd fancied the man earlier, but now he felt decidedly alarmed.

Did they have a madman on their hands?

10

When George got to the library, he gave the driver a dollar tip and ran inside. Then he stood in the lobby, unsure which way to go. Where could Ophie have gone? Why would she even **be** here?

A middle-aged woman came up to him. "Might I help you, sir?"

How to find her? "Um, did you see a young woman?" He measured her height with his hand. "This tall, strawberry blonde, wearing a dark mustard-colored coat and hat."

"I did," the woman said. "She wanted the periodicals." Then she paused, scrutinizing his face. "I hope nothing's amiss?"

She made it here. He took a deep breath, let it out, heart pounding. "Can you show me that section?"

She smiled at him. "I most certainly can."

When he saw Ophie sitting in front of stacks of newspapers, he felt so relieved he thought he might cry. "You're okay!"

"Of course I'm okay," Ophie said. Then she shook herself, glancing around. "Why are **you** here?" Then she gasped. "Gosh. What time is it?"

George looked round: there were no clocks in this room. "It's well after nine. Mrs. Kilpatrick was frantic. The club called —"

Ophie's hands went to her mouth. "I completely lost track of the time."

He plopped himself down and threw his arms around her, head on her shoulder. *She's okay.* "I thought some horrible thing had happened to you."

Ophie put her arms around him. "Oh, my dear Georgie." She sounded touched, and pleased as well. "I'm so sorry to scare you." Then she drew back, turned to the papers. "I couldn't get wanting to know what happened to Pam out of my mind! So I thought that if I came here, I'd find something about it in the papers."

George sat up. "And did you?"

"I found the city news. Lots of tabloids, too." She shook her head. "She was in the middle of a huge scandal! No wonder she doesn't want to go home." Ophie turned pensive. "It looks like it was more than she just got mixed up with the Mob. She went after the Mayor, who it sounds like was **in** the Mob! But this goes **way** back before just a year ago." She surveyed the papers strewn about her. "I can't find the most recent copies."

"I'll help," George said. "What am I looking for?"

She pointed to a large collection of racks, each containing hanging folders stuffed full of old newspapers. "That's the section. Ugh, it took me forever just to find which city, even with the librarian's help."

George felt uneasy. "How much did you tell her?"

Ophie giggled. "I told her I had a project for school."

Whew, George thought. "First let's see what you've got. It might give us some clues."

She began laying out both legitimate newspapers and cheap tabloids, the most recent first, so only the headlines showed:

CITY WATCHES, WRESTLES WITH TRUTH
HOW COULD SHE?
IS MAYOR A VILLAIN?
LIAR, LIAR
MAYOR DENIES EVERY ALLEGATION
THIS MANY LIES?
"MAYOR GAVE ME ENGAGEMENT RING"
HOW OLD <u>WAS</u> SHE?
DOZENS DEAD: MAYOR ACCUSED
AN INDECENT MAN?
ACCUSATIONS GALORE
COMPELLING TESTIMONY

George stared, speechless. "And she was ...?"

"The main one accusing him. But **so** many came forward that I'd be surprised if he wasn't impeached."

"I hadn't heard any of this." A chuckle burst out. "But then, I'm not much for reading the news." And it seemed there were enough scandals right here in Chicago to make up for it. He stood peering at the papers. "It sounds like she was winning! You're right: something had to have gone terribly wrong for her to have run, much less here."

"Well, didn't you read that flier? The one Mr. Hector showed us? It said, 'Wanted for questioning.' I can't imagine the Feds would want to question her unless something absolutely huge happened."

"Yeah," George said absentmindedly. But he couldn't imagine what that might be.

***

Mrs. Jackson stood looking at the cut wires, but she was thinking of what her Mr. Jackson had said: *the murderer is with us.*

But why murder someone at a party in their honor?

A shriek, in the direction of the elevator shaft. One of the twins stood facing the door to the stair, hands to her face. In front of her, his back to the door, stood the young brown-haired waiter Hugh, holding a shiny clean carving knife. "Not gonna let you do it!"

Everyone rushed over.

Mr. Carlo shouted, "Put down that knife, this instant!"

The young man's words were slurred. "You fired me, sir. I'm not yours to command, no more."

"Son," the old man said, hand out. "Come on. You don't want to hurt anyone. Gimme the knife, son."

Hugh's hands went to his sides, his fists balled up. He screamed, "I'm not your **son**!"

Mr. Carlo and the old man rushed him. Instead of fighting, Hugh ran for the pool. A chase began, everyone seemingly wanting to catch him.

But instead of going in the water, he ran past it, past the toilets and the towels, and heaved something small over the edge, which made a jingling noise as it went. Then he dropped the knife, speaking in the group's general direction. "You'll never get away. I won't let you get away with it!"

Mr. Carlo and the old man grabbed Hugh then, marching him over to a table. Mr. Carlo said, "Stay there, you, or we'll tie you to the chair!"

"They can't get away with it," the young man sobbed. "I won't let them do it. No, sir. Not like before."

Mrs. Jackson had followed. "Who?"

Hugh's eyes were red. He made a wild gesture in the direction of the group. "Them."

She peered into the young man's eyes. "Did you call the police? Or did you cut the telephone wire?"

He focused on her. "Both. They're not gonna get away with this."

"Bah," said Mr. Carlo. "Surely we have the murderer right here. He's only trying to pin it on someone else."

Mrs. Jackson straightened. "No. He couldn't have done it. Just look! His shirt is spotless, and he's got not a drop on him. And that knife had no blood on it either."

Mr. Carlo twitched. "You there," he said to Victor. "Get me that knife."

Victor fetched the knife by the very tip of its handle, hand shaking. And sure enough, the blade was as clean as the day was long.

Mrs. Jackson crouched beside Hugh again. "What did you throw over the side?"

"The key to the stair," he said. "They'll not sneak down that way!"

Mrs. Jackson stared at him. Why would he lock the stair? Why did he think the killer was still here? "You said, 'them.' Did you see them do it?

Right at that moment, the lights went out.

11

Ophelia had just found the paper she wanted! Now she couldn't see a thing.

Far off, people shrieked, called out. "Ophie," George said, a quaver in his voice. "Are you okay?"

"I'm okay." She felt a bit scared. "But I can't see."

His words were kind. "Come to my voice."

The table was in the way. Papers rustled to the floor. She felt round until she found him, and sat beside him.

He grabbed her hand. "How are we going to get out of here?"

She shrugged, then realized he couldn't see her. "I don't know. But I wonder why the lights failed." She pondered that for a moment. "If there were windows, we could see if we're the only ones without power."

"That's a good question," George said. "Do they have a generator? Even candles would do. Although I can't see wanting flame around a building full of paper."

Ophelia giggled at the idea.

George said, "Maybe we should wait for someone to come get us. Or for the light to go back on. I don't remember the way here."

"Okay." She liked holding George's hand.

After a while, he said, "Did you get what you needed?"

"I suppose. But the most recent news from that city is gone. I wonder why?"

George got quiet for a while. "I know you just want to help. But what if Hector and Pamela are keeping things quiet to protect us?"

"What do you mean?"

She could hear him take a deep, shaky breath, let it out. "Someone's **after** them! What if those guys took the papers to see who comes looking?"

Ophelia tried to figure what he meant. "You mean, like a signal?"

"Yeah. Why would someone go looking for that specific person, about something that happened all that way away, more than a year ago? They'd have to have a reason." He fell silent again, just for a bit. "It'd be easy to set a man in every big city, have him frequent the libraries, the records hall, and wait for some palooka to take the bait."

Ophelia felt scared. "So what do I do?"

George let out another breath. "Let it alone. You found what you wanted. You know there was a scandal. You know people are after her, people mean enough to kill her husband and son. They either think she knows something and want to shut her up, or they think she did something and want revenge for it." A rustling sound, as if he moved. "I don't know which, and neither does Hector. But he's spending **way** too much on a place for them to run to at the very **thought** of these people finding her." He got quiet for a minute. "I don't think it's the Feds."

"Who else would it be?"

"Well, somebody in the Mob's after them too, right? Back where they come from."

"Ohhh." She wasn't scared of the Feds, not really. They were government guys. But ... "You're scared they're going to come after us."

"Yeah."

So she and George either had to go with Pam and Mr. Hector, or stay here and hope the men didn't find them. "What do you want to do?"

He took a deep breath. "I'm staying. I can't leave my parents like that, just disappear. Besides, if these guys figure out I knew them, they'd go after my parents. I can't leave them here to face that alone. They have no idea what's going on."

She never even thought of that. If they couldn't find her, would these men go after Mrs. Kilpatrick, the girls at the boarding house, the girls at Club Patruni?

It scared her. She didn't know what to do. She still didn't have an answer to Mr. Hector's question. And she felt like she should. "Sometimes I don't think Pam really cares about me."

George got quiet for a while. "I think she cares about you a whole lot."

"But —"

"The problem's not that she doesn't love you. The problem's that she's scared to."

This felt like someone punched her in the chest, and for a minute, she couldn't breathe. After her mom died, she felt like that for a long while. She felt cold inside, empty. And then a woman followed her into an alley.

Pam. She'd never met anyone like her.

"At least, that's what Hector thinks," George said, "and I agree. He doesn't know any more than you do, and he married her anyway, because he loves her." He got quiet, then chuckled softly.

"What's funny?"

"Oh, just the goofy smile he gets when he talks about her. But you know what he said? That he was never, ever gonna say he loved her, because that's when he'd wake up to find her gone."

She felt dismayed. "Gosh. I wish I would've known that earlier!" Is that why Pam hadn't come by this whole week, or telephoned her?

Had she made a huge mistake?

George's voice startled her. "What happened with Ethel?"

"What do you mean?"

"Mrs. Kilpatrick said you got a call from her. Before you left for work."

The "Yeah. Her mother's making her get married to the man that she went behind the theater with."

"Does she want to marry him?"

Ethel had been crying. "She doesn't know. She thinks he might be trifling with her."

"That doesn't sound good."

"She doesn't know what to do. She's twenty-four and still not married. And now this. Her mother's worried for her safety if news of it should get out."

"Oh." George sounded surprised. Then he snorted. "Sounds a bit too much like me."

"What do you mean?"

"Heh," he said. "My parents are trying to make me get married, too."

"To who?"

"It's not like **that**. They just want me to settle down."
He laughed. "I suppose to them, anyone would do."

"I'm sorry." Then something came to her. "You were at work!"

"Yeah."

"Won't you get in trouble?"

He let out a laugh. "Probably."

"So why'd you come after me?"

He got real quiet then. "I thought something happened to you."

Oh, boy, she thought. Was **that** what this was all about? "Please, Georgie. Don't get stuck on me." She felt sad. "I told you. Back at the park. I'm not the kind of girl who can give you what you want."

He chuckled. "It's not like that. I like you. We have fun together." He rustled around, then said, "I don't **need** anything from you! All I want is to be around you. I want to take **care** of you, make sure you're okay!" He got quiet for a minute, and when he spoke next he sounded excited. "It'll be swell! Between the two of us, we'll have plenty of dough. Go dancing every night we can, and maybe travel with Pam and Hector someday!" His voice turned like he thought of something funny. "They'll probably be here a while yet. And when they go, maybe we can find someone new."

The thought of Pam leaving gave her a lump in her throat. She would marry Pam herself, if such a thing were ever possible. She squeezed his hand. "I hope they never go. But ... you really want me? Like I am?"

He had a smile in his voice. "You're perfect, Ophie. Exactly the way you are."

12

The sky held waves of green. Mrs. Jackson had never seen such a thing in her life.

On the rooftop of the Myriad Hotel, the group sat in a circle under the light of the torches, seemingly above the chaos that must be going on below.

"My grandmother told me of this," the old woman said. "Hasn't happened here in a hundred years."

The reporter took out his notepad and began scribbling, while the photographer twisted around trying to take pictures of the sky.

"They're called auroras," the old man said. "Caused by the sun, they think. Although I don't know why we're seeing them here. They're supposed to only be up North."

No one had an answer.

Bessie seemed not to mind their new sky one bit. She lay curled beside Mrs. Jackson's right foot, eyes closed.

Ruby pulled her towel around her, sounding afraid. "Why don't the elevators work?"

Russell took off his spectacles and wiped them on his apron. Then he gestured at the electric lights, which were cold and quiet. "They run on power."

Mr. Jackson leaned over to whisper in her ear. "The door to the stair is locked, and the only key available's on the street. How are we going to get down?"

"Well," she whispered back. "If this fellow did call the police, they'll figure out a way to us. I can't imagine old Nestor taking this as anything but a challenge."

He laughed.

Mrs. Von Bilten snapped, "What could you possibly find funny?"

Bessie twitched, letting out a yelp, and looked around before settling back in.

Mrs. Jackson felt contrite. "Nothing. We were just saying that if young Hugh here did call the police, well, we happen to know the man who'd arrive. He'd take getting up here as a challenge."

Cornelius Ober laughed, as did young Charles.

The musicians looked at each other. "Police?"

Bessie's ears went up.

"A man's been killed," said Mr. Carlo. "He's in the greenhouse there. Nothing to be alarmed at. We'll have to make do until the police arrive."

The saxophonist said, "What do you want us to do?"

Everyone looked to Mr. Carlo, who shrugged.

Mrs. Jackson pointed to Hugh. "He threw the key to the stairs over the side. We might just have to wait."

The rest looked various forms of disgruntled.

Mrs. Jackson said, "Forgive me, but I don't actually know many of your names."

"Ah." The Bohemian rose and bowed. "Cornelius Ober at your service." He sat then gesturing to the blonde beside him. "And this magnificent gem is Miss Millicent Book."

"Call me Millie." She beamed. "I'm a singer."

Mrs. Jackson pointed to the actress sitting beside the young woman. "And you are?"

She raised an eyebrow. "Rather chagrined that you don't know!"

"I'm so sorry," Mrs. Jackson said. "We're not from around here."

Mr. Jackson said, "I suppose I've been remiss. I should've taken you to more cinema."

The actress smiled to herself. "Well, in any case, I'm Ada Leb."

Millie gushed, "Only the bee's knees!" She turned to Ada, face aglow. "I never thought I'd get to shake your hand! And here you are, Miss Ada Leb, actually sitting beside me!"

Mrs. Von Bilten sneered. "Alvira Lebensohl, you mean. Born to a back-alley butcher and his cheap dance-hall whore."

Ada raised her chin, unruffled. "Every actress has a stage name. My real name is public record. Say what you like about my parents, but they taught me manners, which is more than I can say for you."

Charles snorted.

Mrs. Jackson admired Ada's courage. "And who is your lucky young man?"

Ada's fiance tipped his fedora, then took Ada's hand. "Ernest Lock, ma'am."

"A pleasure," Mrs. Jackson said. She turned to the old man. "And you are?"

"Lewis McKenney." Mr. McKenney seemed both impatient and disgruntled by the whole affair.

The musicians were Sidney Nanton (the pianist), Otis Zachery on the saxophone, and Maurice Foots on the trumpet. Perry Young played the string bass, and Dennis Edmond the drums. The reporter was Bence Gereben, a strange little thin man. The photographer was named Walter Margin.

"Thank you," Mrs. Jackson said. "We're Pamela and Hector Jackson." She picked up her little dog, snuggling her close. "And this sweet girl is Bessie."

A round of "how do you do", and most smiled at little Bessie before Mrs. Jackson returned her to the floor.

Except for Mrs. Von Bilten. She snapped, "How is this nonsense going to find his killer?"

Mrs. Jackson shrugged. "I've no idea. But I like to know who I'm speaking with." Then Mrs. Jackson raised her voice. "Young lady, you can come out now."

Silence, for an uncomfortable amount of time — Mrs. Jackson hoped she hadn't been wrong — then a woman who looked precisely like Ruby emerged into the torches' glow from the direction of the elevator shaft, still clutching her golden towel.

Mr. Jackson gasped. "I never suspected!"

Millie said matter-of-factly, "They're famous. Always getting into some sort of trouble."

Chin held high, the young woman approached the group as if her double wasn't sitting right there. Victor got her a chair, the others scooted over, and she sat, not looking at anyone.

Mr. Jackson said, "However did you guess?"

"Just look at them," said Mrs. Jackson. She pointed at the newcomer. "I knew the minute I saw her, back in the greenhouse after the murder. A woman having been pushed into a pool would have her hair and makeup ruined. Yet this one's hair only wetted, not soaked. And her makeup is perfect."

The twins glared at each other.

Mr. Jackson chuckled. "And it seems the 'one-of-a-kind' dress has its pair."

Mr. Carlo scowled.

"**I'm** Ruby," Perfect Makeup said. "Not her."

Mrs. Jackson turned to the other girl, who, while dried off, still looked somewhat like a drowned rat. "Then who are **you**?"

The girl snorted. "You really **aren't** from around here, are you? Pearl Carlisle, at your service."

Mr. Jackson laughed. "Ah. Oyster."

Cornelius Ober chuckled.

"Hmm," said Mrs. Jackson. "So why pretend?"

"I was doing an interview downstairs," said the real Ruby. "I was the one invited, and I didn't want to cause a scene by arriving late. So I sent Pearl in my place."

"I don't think so," Mrs. Jackson and Mr. Carlo said.

They looked at each other.

"You were both invited," said Mr. Carlo. "Mr. Rothmore insisted."

Pearl laughed. "Why would we lie about **that**?"

"I don't know," Mrs. Jackson said. "But Ruby has your real mole drawn on." She turned to Ruby. "So Ruby, you were pretending to be **her**, not the other way round." She leaned back. "Which makes me wonder: why would Miss Pearl want to be up here so badly?"

Pearl glanced away, drawing her towel around her. "I despise interviews."

Cornelius Ober said dryly, "Yet you give so many of them."

Pearl rolled her eyes.

"And in each one," Mr. Ober said, "you talk about your father's work. Touching."

"He was a great man," Pearl said.

"My condolences," said Mr. Ober. He looked around. "I think we all feel the same."

"Wait," Mr. Jackson said. "Your father died?"

"Several weeks ago," Mr. Gereben said. "It was in the papers." He preened, just a bit. "I did the story myself. The result of injuries sustained in the War."

Mr. Ober scoffed.

Both the twins looked away.

"Oh, I'm so sorry," Mrs. Jackson said quickly.

Hugh let out a soft snore.

Mrs. Jackson pointed to the sleeping young waiter. "Does anyone know what he was going on about?"

Russell said, "Not exactly. But he's been acting nervous ever since," he gestured with his chin at Pearl, "that one arrived."

Mr. Jackson leaned forward. "Nervous?"

Mr. McKenney snorted. "Sure acting strangely for a man in love."

"No," Russell said. "Not nervous like that. Like he was scared of her. Or angry, and didn't know what to do about it."

Mrs. Jackson said, "Pearl, he said something to you when he got you your drink. What was it?"

Pearl shrugged. "Must not have been anything worth remembering, because I can't recall." She laughed. "That **was** several drinks ago." She went quiet. "I knew him back in school. He's always been twitchy." She looked around at everyone. "I got nothing against him. I even bought him a drink."

Victor nodded, his long bangs falling across his face. "I remember: she did."

Mrs. Jackson thought through what she'd seen, heard. "Whoever killed this man did so with a knife. Yet not only is our very drunk waiter's shirt flawless, the knife he brandished is clean. So —"

"I suppose he might've changed his shirt and washed up," Mr. Ober said.

The old man said, "I wonder. What marks might you find on **that** outlandish suit?"

Everyone looked. Every bit Mr. Cornelius Ober wore was dark, down to his calf-high black leather boots. Perfect for hiding blood.

It was then she noticed a large deep red spot staining the embroidery of his floor-length coat, at about the level of his knee.

Pearl had venom in her tone. "Everyone knows you hate the man."

Mr. Ober laughed. "Nonsense. I was by the banister giving an interview with our reporter and photographer here," he gestured at the men, who nodded, "when someone said they heard screaming." He glanced at the others. "I presume that's when you found the body?"

Mr. Jackson said, "It was."

Charles pointed to the man's coat. "What's that stain from, then?"

Cornelius Ober peered down. "This?" He chuckled. "A bit too much fun three parties ago. My wash lady never could remove the stain. But I adore this coat simply too much to get rid of it."

Mrs. Jackson said, "Mr. Ober, why do you hate Mr. Rothmore? What's he done?"

The man crossed his legs at the knee and looked away, taking a drag from his cigarette on its long holder before blowing a smoke-ring. "Nothing I can prove, mind you. But every time one of us would do a showing, a pane or three would be broken." He shrugged. "Happened to me more than once."

Mr. Jackson leaned forward. "And you blamed him."

"Everyone did," Ruby said. "He never had anything broken, ever."

Well, Mrs. Jackson thought. This surely **was** personal. And more than a bit ironic. "It seems we all have alibis for the crime. But if you recall, the man was dragged to where we found him. Bags of stone were then dropped upon him —"

The old woman flinched.

"— and the scene was tidied up. That took time. And some strength. And balancing on a ladder as you push over a fifty-pound bag of stone? It isn't easy. So —"

The trumpet player Mr. Foots looked incredulous. "Wait just a minute. Bags of **stone**?"

Old Mr. McKenney said, "The same."

Mr. Foots put his hand upon his forehead. "Mercy. That poor man."

Mr. Carlo snapped, "You lot go back there and play." With the torches and candles, the lighting was dimmer than before, but good enough. "I'll not have you sit here when I'm paying you."

The five band members looked at each other, got up in a resigned manner, and returned to their posts. After a minute or so, soft music wafted overhead.

Soon one person wanted a drink, another something to eat, and the group dissipated.

Cornelius Ober and Millie began a slow dance. Mr. Lock and Ada Leb moved to a table and began quietly conversing. Mr. McKenney got another drink, then lit his pipe, facing Victor in an apparent discussion.

Russell checked on the buffet. He then went to the photographer, Mr. Margin, and began conversing. Mr. Margin opened a large flat case he had with him and took out one of the many portfolios inside.

Mrs. Von Bilten sat crying. Charles made an attempt to console her, but she said something which seemed to offend him. The young man threw his arms up and went to the banister, standing between the jazz band and the greenhouse.

Mrs. Jackson, Mr. Jackson, and Mr. Carlo stood in the middle of the party area. Bessie lay curled up beside Mrs. Jackson's feet.

The pool was only faintly lit by the guttering votives encircling it. Between those and their better-lit area lay only darkness.

Hugh still slept, his head on his arms upon the table. Mrs. Jackson was reminded of their last case, the man shot dead in the speakeasy.

She said to Mr. Carlo, "I think this young man either knew something, or saw something. I'd very much like to have a talk with him when he awakens."

"I'm sure the police will too," Mr. Carlo said. "Threatening guests with a knife? Public drunkenness?" He shook his head. "And he seemed such a decent sort."

Mr. Jackson said, "What do you mean?"

Mr. Carlo chuckled. "We check the background of our new hires. They're dealing with money and personal items, after all." He gestured at the young man. "College man. He was on the varsity swimming team."

Mrs. Jackson said, "Was?"

Mr. Carlo shook his head. "He's taking a year off. A death of someone close to him. A roommate, I believe. He wouldn't get into detail about it. And then the year before, his father passed away."

"Poor fellow," Mr. Jackson said. "He's evidently gone into paranoia."

Mr. Carlo gazed up at the swirling green overhead. "Maybe I was too hard on the lad." Then he let out a laugh. "Too bad he threw the key over the side."

Mrs. Jackson said, "Might it not have landed on the lower level?"

"Heh," Mr. Carlo said. "I wish. But the heave-to the boy gave that thing? It's probably across the street."

Mr. Jackson shrugged. "Take heart. It's considerably more comfortable here than in the stairwell."

"Well," Mrs. Jackson said, "don't forget our suite is only the one floor below."

"Yes," Mr. Jackson said. "But even if we could get down there, we'd have half this lot — plus Sergeant Nestor — in our suite for the rest of the night."

Mr. Carlo laughed. "True enough." He looked over at them. "So perhaps it turned out for the best. Care for some refreshments?"

Mrs. Jackson got some tea; her Mr. Jackson chose coffee. Interested in the photography, she strolled over to where Mr. Margin sat.

The man glanced up when they approached. "Care to join me?"

Mr. Jackson said, "Certainly."

So they sat.

Mrs. Jackson said, "Do you accompany Mr. Gereben often?"

He laughed. "I work with whoever hires me. Mostly society affairs, such as this one." He took out a business card and handed it over. Then his mood soured. "I've done work involving Mr. Rothmore before."

Mr. Jackson said, "You make it sound unpleasant."

Mr. Margin sighed. "Well, he could be a capricious and yes, unpleasant man."

Mrs. Jackson said, "Whatever do you mean?"

Mr. Margin hesitated, then drew a second portfolio from his large case, opening it onto the table. "I'd done a spread — at his request — to show as part of a photography exhibit. I'd entered the exhibit at my own cost, and was planning to sell some of the prints there." He fell silent.

Mr. Jackson leaned forward, "What happened?"

"I'd sent the spread over for his review the day before the show. I thought he might want to take out one or maybe two. Sometimes in these cases, that happens. But he telephoned that night, saying he was withdrawing his entire exhibit. He insisted on keeping every photo! But of course I'd made copies." His shoulders drooped. "I can't sell them without his permission, but I can show others my work." He crossed his arms in front of him. "I was out fifty dollars for the entry fee. I wouldn't have come to this affair at all, but Bence is a friend. The photographer he'd hired cancelled at the last minute."

Mrs. Jackson felt curious. "Might I see these photos?"

The photographer shrugged, sliding the portfolio towards her.

The pictures were quite ordinary: the greenhouse, the architect standing before it. Most were of lush plants, fountains, the effects of light being cast upon the ground. But there was one of the architect bent over, speaking with two small boys. Or rather, by his stance, scolding them. "Where was this taken?"

"Around back of the greenhouse." He peered at the scene. "This was at a model showing. Dozens of greenhouse designers made small glass houses for the event. I believe this was outside one of the others."

From the look of it, Mr. Rothmore seemed disapproving, perhaps even angry. "I wonder what was going on here."

"He gave those boys a good talking-to. But I never learned what for."

13

Leaving the party behind and Bessie with Mr. Jackson, Mrs. Jackson took one of the tapered candles and made her way into the darkness between the party area and the water. She then threaded past the guttering votives along the pool to the Ladies' Room.

She was at once faced with where to put the candle. Finally, she dripped some of the wax onto the floor and stood the base of the candle up in it.

It was late; she felt weary. As she sat staring at the flame, her mind returned to Mr. Rothmore, still lying dead in the greenhouse.

His death surely felt personal.

Ruby — or rather, Pearl — said they all hated each other. Perhaps enough to murder?

The hulking bodyguard and his actress had an alibi — the young blonde.

And neither had motive to kill the man.

The Bohemian had motive. But he had an alibi — the photographer and reporter.

The old woman seemed devastated at the architect's death; it seemed she'd had some feeling for the man.

Mr. McKenney had been with her and Bessie when they found the body. The musicians had been playing at the time.

Mr. Carlo, of course, had no motive whatsoever. He hated scandal at his hotel, and this was nothing but.

So who did that leave?

A huge amount of splashing, right outside. Were they really playing around the pool again?

After some time, the splashing quieted, stopped.

Then footsteps. Then a shriek!

A woman cried, "Help! Help!"

Mrs. Jackson stood, arranged her clothing, picked up the candle, and made her way outside.

All of the men, including the musicians, were hurrying across the rooftop towards them.

One of the twins stood there, hands to her mouth, staring at the water.

Hugh floated in watery darkness, face down.

14

As the men arrived, Mrs. Jackson pointed to the man in the water. One of the musicians took off his jacket, handed it to another, then dove in.

Her Mr. Jackson rushed to her side, Bessie bounding beside him. "Are you hurt?"

She shook her head and picked up Bessie. "I just came out here."

The musician flipped the man over and began pulling the unmoving figure back to the steps. The other men pulled the limp man out of the water and turned him face down.

The women trailed up more slowly, gasping when they saw the dead man lying there.

"I know resuscitation," Cornelius Ober said. "You there," he pointed to Victor. "This takes two. Keep his arms near to the pavers, then move them above his head." He crouched, demonstrating, and the waiter followed. "Then quickly down." He moved the arm he held down to the man's side. "We must act in unison. Let's do it again. Up, and down. Up, and down."

The pair continued on.

Russell nodded approvingly. "I've seen this before. They do this at the lake for drownings."

Mrs. Jackson had never seen the technique before. "Did it work?"

The blond waiter looked startled. "It seemed to."

"Lift his legs," Mr. McKenney said, "so the water may drain out."

Victor tried to do so, but it seemed Hugh's legs were too heavy. With a growl, the old man took one of the legs, lifting Hugh's hips above his chest. A gush of water came from the young man's mouth.

Mr. Carlo knelt beside Hugh and began pounding his back in various places. "The nurses do this for fluid on the lungs."

Mrs. Jackson nodded. Duchess Cordelia had helped her in just this way when she had a bad case of bronchitis after the New Year.

The rest encouraged them on.

But after some time, fatigue on their faces, they stopped. Mr. Ober felt for a pulse, and shook his head.

Mrs. Jackson hugged Bessie, feeling devastated. Possibly the one man who might tell what he'd seen, and now he was dead!

Mr. Carlo said to the girl who'd found him, "Why didn't you get him out?"

Drops glittered on the young woman's cheeks under flawless makeup. "I tried. I went in. But he was too far out, and I don't know how to swim!"

Good thing **she** wasn't pushed into the pool, Mrs. Jackson thought. "Did you see what happened?"

"I was on my way to the Ladies' Room. But I couldn't see anything but the candles," she pointed, "down here." The beaded edge of her dark brown dress dripped. "Then I heard the splashing," she pointed, "and so I came around over here. Then I saw his shirt, and it moved. Good gracious, it startled me!"

Mr. Jackson leaned over to whisper in Mrs. Jackson's ear. "Something's not right."

She nodded. Then she called out, "Let's cover him up and leave him be. The police will be here soon enough."

***

Ophelia still sat in the library, darkness all around, holding hands with George.

What he'd suggested didn't seem real. Him and her, together? She supposed he wanted to marry.

Men just weren't like that: they wanted regular women, not someone like her.

Was George lying about her being all right for him? Did he think he was going to **change** her?

No. She couldn't live like that. She wouldn't.

She let go of George's hand, staring into the darkness. What should she do?

Somehow, her Mama knew the influenza was taking her. And she worried so much as she lay dying. "Bad times are coming, little girl. I can feel it. Just promise me you'll marry. Promise me you'll find a man that'll keep you safe."

But what could she say? She'd never found a man she wanted ... like that. The thought of a man pawing at her felt repulsive.

Maybe it wouldn't be so bad. George wasn't like most men. He was kind and good-natured and sensible. He wanted to take her dancing, and travel the world. He cared about her, and about what she wanted, too.

Pam wasn't going to stay here, whether she went with her or not. And it seemed like the more she tried to push Pam to talk, the more she pulled away. Even that time Pam said her real name seemed to upset her, make her scared.

If what George said was true, maybe she shouldn't be looking for the truth. Maybe it was going to cause more harm than good.

But there, alone in the dark, the truth crept up to her on its own. She could almost hear her Mama speak: *It's time to grow up, baby girl.*

She was twenty-one and a full adult woman. Pam had been through one of the most awful things a woman could imagine. Being held up to public scandal? Called a liar? Then to see her husband and child dead?

She shuddered.

And looking back on what she'd done of the past week, how she'd acted ...

Ophelia felt ashamed of herself.

Maybe instead of badgering Pam and going behind her back, she should have been looking for ways to make Pam's life better. Like Mr. Hector was doing. Instead, she'd been acting like a spoiled child demanding more than Pam might ever be able to give.

George's voice startled her. "I'll tell you everything, Ophie. Everything. Even about me and Hector." He squeezed her hand tight, but only for a moment. "I promise."

She felt entirely confused. Her heart was pounding so loud she thought sure he could hear it. "Wait. You ... and Mr. Hector?"

He sounded like he was smiling. "Of course, silly. Didn't you know?" She heard him breathe in, and it wobbled. "I'll tell you everything. Everything. And you can tell me everything, too."

She didn't know why, or how, or even when, but she found herself with her arms around him, sobbing into his jacket.

George was like **her**!

She didn't have to hide who she was anymore, be scared anymore. Worry about anyone leaving her anymore. And now, there in the dark with her friend, it seemed like everything was finally going to be all right.

15

The group returned to the chairs. Mrs. Jackson felt grieved and disturbed. Mr. Jackson was right: this didn't happen naturally. And the story Ruby gave made no sense.

Hugh had clearly seen something he shouldn't, something he'd been killed to silence. Why would anyone kill a waiter, otherwise?

He'd been trying to tell them what was going on this entire time. He thought he knew who killed Mr. Rothmore, someone he feared would get away with the crime "like last time." But he'd been so intoxicated nothing **he**'d said made sense.

The exchange she'd seen between Hugh and Pearl, well before the first murder, felt suspicious.

But there seemed to be no connection (at least, that she'd seen) between the young waiter and Ruby. If she did hurt him, why?

No one wanted music anymore, so the musicians (along with Mr. Foots holding his own golden towel) joined the rest at the circle.

Mr. Edmond (Mrs. Jackson thought he was the drummer. Or was he the bassist?) said, "Why aren't the police here already?"

Mr. McKenney got out his pipe. "If that waiter really did call them, they might've gotten stuck in the elevator when the power went out."

Mr. Carlo kept shaking his head. "How did he get into the pool? Why wasn't anyone watching him?"

Mrs. Jackson said, "You really think he wandered over there and fell in on his own?"

Mr. Nanton had been sitting leaned over, staring at a folder of piano music in his hand. "It's certainly possible. It's dark, and the toilets are that way. He was so drunk he might have forgotten about the pool."

A bit of silence, then Mr. Lock said, "I meant to watch over him. But he was asleep. Me and Ada got to talking, and I thought he'd stay asleep, at least for a while." He sighed. "I just don't see how he could've gotten all that way by himself."

Mr. Carlo persisted. "There are twenty of us here at least. No one saw him get up? Walk, what is it, thirty yards to the pool?"

Everyone glanced at each other, shook their heads.

Mr. Jackson looked abashed. "I admit, I've been most distracted this evening." He looked around at the rest. "A business deal."

Ada looked at her Mr. Lock, then back at the group. "We've been talking of the best way to break this to our parents. The engagement." She glanced aside. "They're not fond of the match."

"Corny and I were dancing," Millie said.

The musicians glanced at each other and shrugged. "We was playin', like you told us to," Mr. Zachery said.

Ruby they'd all seen. Mrs. Jackson turned to Pearl, who'd wiped most of the makeup off of her cheeks. "What were you doing all this time?"

"She was with me," Charles said. "Over at the banister. Having a drink. Whatever you might think of the situation, these auroras make one hell of a show."

Mrs. Von Bilten cried out, "Don't you care **anything** about him being **dead**?"

Everyone turned to stare at her.

Mrs. Jackson said, "Him? Which him?"

She clasped her hands to her mouth, appalled.

"Heh," Charles said. "Now you've done it."

Mrs. Jackson peered at the old woman for a moment. Then it came to her. "Lydia **Rothman** Von Bilten —"

The old woman flinched.

"You're a relation, aren't you? But you don't like it that I say so. Why is it?"

Mrs. Von Bilten said, "They should **never** have printed that! I told them to change it, but they said it was too late."

Millie said, "What's wrong with you being related? He's a big name!"

"Yeah," Mr. Zachery said. "I'da thought you'd be proud."

Mr. Gereben was scribbling furiously.

Mrs. Von Bilten turned on him. "Stop that this instant! I'll not have a spectacle made of his death!"

Mrs. Jackson said, "You mean a scandal." She knew very well about scandals. "You've been making a spectacle of yourself this entire time. Do **you** know what's going on here? Who is Mr. Rothmore to you?"

"I'd like to know myself," said Mr. Carlo, his face severe. "It's **my** hotel being dragged through the papers. If you know why this man was killed, speak up now."

The old woman's face turned angry. She pointed at Mrs. Jackson. "You." Then she pointed at Mr. Carlo. "The both of you. You should be ashamed of yourselves!" Then she pointed at Mrs. Jackson, and the hate on her face made Mrs. Jackson quail. "Pamela Jackson, indeed." She scoffed. "Young lady, I know **exactly** who you are."

16

George heard footsteps, then the light of a lantern burst upon the scene. Ophie jerked upright and away from him.

"Oh, ho!" A man's voice, sarcasm dripping. "Look what we have here!" He looked back at the group of younger men and women behind him, most holding lanterns. "Young lovers, taking advantage of the night."

George stood. "It's nothing of the sort." He offered Ophie his hand, and she took it. "Come on, let's go."

A lantern had been set on the floor down the hall, at the corner. Hoots and jeers followed George and Ophelia as they went.

Ophie sounded frantic. "We gotta get out of here before word gets to Mrs. Kilpatrick!"

Once they got out of sight of the group, he stopped, faced her. "Nothing bad'll happen." Although with the lantern on the floor behind her he couldn't see her face, he smiled at her anyway. "I have a plan."

Using the lanterns to guide him, George led Ophie to the exit. Outside, all was chaos: some running in the darkness, others staring at the bright green ribbons in the sky, which George had never seen before. Car horns honked. A man screamed over and over that the world was ending.

Other than a bit of light from the ribbons, it was near pitch out. The headlights of automobiles gave off the only real light, making it even harder to see anything after they passed in the darkness.

George flagged down a taxi. "The Myriad Hotel, on the double."

Once the taxi set off for the Hotel, George said to Ophie, "If the power's out here, it's out there, too. I left Will with over a hundred guests at dinner, and he might need our help."

***

Bessie started barking at the old woman.

The couple looked at each other, fear in their faces. If Mrs. Von Bilten knew who Mrs. Jackson really was, what would she do?

Mrs. Jackson wanted to run, to hide. But there was nowhere to run, and she refused to hide any longer. "What is it you think you know about me?"

The old lady scowled. "You're nothing but a cheap gold-digging guttersnipe playing as an investigator that has latched on to one rich man after another. You killed your first husband when it suited you —"

A knife went through her heart. Her eyes stung.

"— and I wouldn't put it past you to be plotting this one's death as well."

Mr. Jackson picked up Bessie, who had been barking and growling the entire time. "That is both decidedly unkind and entirely wrong." He smoothed the little dog's hair. "Hush, dear: all is well."

The old woman pointed at Mrs. Jackson, "**You** were the one to find Horace dead! What is it **you** know about his death, hmm?"

To her surprise, Mrs. Jackson no longer felt afraid. "I'm learning more with every word from your mouth. Why do you not want to tell us about your relationship with 'Horace'? If you care about him, why **wouldn't** you want the truth to come out? Why attack those who want the truth? We've seen you out here all evening making a show of your grief, but you're a rich woman with connections. Of course you wouldn't kill him **yourself**!"

Charles let out an ironic chuckle.

"So ma'am, I have to ask. Did you **have** him killed?"

The woman looked horrified. "**Me?** No! Why would I? I **loved** him!"

Several of the men said, "Ohhh!" Their faces were both amused and more than a bit scandalized.

"You don't understand!" The old woman looked close to tears. "You can't possibly understand."

Charles put his hand on her arm. "Grandma, sooner or later you're going to have to tell them."

Mrs. Von Bilten's head drooped. "Very well." She took a deep breath; her voice shook. "Horace wasn't my lover. He was ..." She hesitated a long time. "My son."

17

The entire group stared at her, and you could have heard a pin drop.

Charles handed her a handkerchief, and she wiped her eyes. "I was young and foolish, and got into an entirely unsuitable affair. My parents covered it up after I gave birth, and they sent Horace away. But he was my baby! I loved him! I secretly helped him any way I might. I put him through school, gave him connections. He was a great man —"

Her grandson scoffed.

Mrs. Jackson held up a hand. "Wait. Mr. De Rege, are you Mr. Rothmore's son?"

"Hardly," Charles said. "I'm the legitimate one." He shook his head. "My mother was **never** good enough. She was hounded out of the house, and married a man my grandmother hated."

"Now, Charles —"

"It's true. Just like my mother. My father wasn't rich enough, he wasn't good enough. Not like her darling Horace! Now that they're dead, I'm being pressured to become some rich thing." He scoffed. "I hate it all." He gestured at Cornelius Ober. "**He** lives as he pleases, does what he likes —!"

Mr. Jackson laughed. "My guess is he's rich as well."

"By doing what he loves!" He turned to Mr. Ober. "Am I right?"

Cornelius Ober took his cigarette from his mouth. "That you are, sir."

Charles De Rege stood, throwing his arms in the air. "I spit on it all! The lies, the deception, the obligation." He pointed back at his grandmother. "Did you know she hired boys to throw those rocks?"

Everyone gasped. Ruby's eyes filled with tears.

His grandmother turned on him in a fury. "Charles!"

"Well, she did. She's all but bankrupted him, pushing him to do one foolish thing after another."

Pearl stood, pointing at Mrs. Von Bilten with a shaking hand. "You harpy! You ruined my father, drove him to his grave!"

Cornelius Ober shook his head. "I **knew** that story about your father dying of his 'war injuries' was false! For one, he never went."

Mr. McKenney said, "He didn't?"

"No," said Mr. Ober. He chuckled. "Just a bit too old to go marching off to this last one, wouldn't you say?"

"Well," Mrs. Von Bilten said, "I always assumed they meant the one before."

"No," said Pearl. "He killed himself. He tried and tried to make his business work. He was a genius! Yet he never got a chance. After you hounded him, broke his priceless works, then stole his inventions ... it became too much." She pointed to herself. "**My** father was first to put in the mechanical timers for the upper windows — but **you** made sure that story was squashed. And when your darling boy put his in, you made sure it was the talk of the town. We did **everything** to help him ..." her voice broke, and she slumped into her chair, putting her face in her hands.

Mrs. Jackson had the feeling of a revelation, without the words or meaning coming to her. Her heart pounded, her hands shook.

The reporter took out a second notepad.

Mrs. Jackson's voice shook. "So you and your sister **killed** him!"

Ruby gasped. "I never meant him **harm**! But Pearl said go do the interview, then meet her at the back of the greenhouse. When I got there ..." She began to tremble. "Oh, it was horrible! Pearl said we had to make it look an accident. So —"

The thought was right there, but she couldn't find it. Couldn't see it. What was it?

Mr. Jackson seemed to be looking at Bessie's back. "You helped her. Dragged him over, cleaned the plants, pushed over the bags of stone."

"What else could I do? She's my **sister**! Could I just let her go to **jail**?"

Mr. Carlo blurted out, "Did you send those boys to throw rocks at my greenhouse the other week?"

This shocked her. Had Pearl known they'd attend this event even **then**? That proved planning beyond what she'd even imagined.

Pearl said, "Thought it'd be good to give him a taste of his own medicine. But they went much too early."

The connection between the waiter and the architect must be these girls. Mrs. Jackson felt angry. "**That's** why you jumped into the pool!"

Mr. Carlo was astonished. "What? The boy was telling the truth?"

Mrs. Jackson felt shaky. "He was. Am I right?"

Pearl said, "So what if he was?"

Mr. Jackson's head rose. "Ah. Yes. He saw you come out of the back of the greenhouse. Cutting someone's throat is messy, even botching it like you did."

Ruby said, "B-botched? But he **died**!"

"After some time," said Mr. Jackson. "No, if she'd brought in a professional, Mr. Rothmore would've been dead long before we arrived." He faced Pearl. "In any case, you had to have been covered in blood. And the waiter saw you. So you did the only reasonable thing: jumped in to wash it off, then framed him for it."

Mrs. Jackson crossed her arms, grieved. And angry. "And an innocent man is now disgraced and dead." But the question still lingered ... She turned to Ruby. "What do you say to that?"

Ruby held a drink, but her hands shook. "I had to keep him quiet! He was going to ruin everything."

And Mrs. Jackson thought of her husband that night he died. He had everything a man could want: a beautiful home, a wife who loved him, a son ...

Why confront them, when he knew they had guns?

Mr. Jackson leaned forward and spoke kindly. "Dear girl, what did you do?"

Ruby only stared at her drink.

Pearl said, "I put some of my Veronal powder in his champagne. When I gave it to him. He'd come by me and said, 'I have my eye on you!' Well —"

Mrs. Jackson's confusion distracted her from the insight she felt coming to her. "Wait. Veronal?"

"It's a sleeping powder," Mr. Carlo said.

"Oh," said Mrs. Jackson.

Pearl sneered. "You really **aren't** from around here!"

Mrs. Jackson snorted. The girl had no idea. "Never you mind." She turned to Ruby. "But that was well before your sister killed Mr. Rothman. Why did he suspect you even then?"

Mr. McKenney blurted, "Where's my **money**? He was going into the greenhouse to get my money!"

Pearl laughed. "Where you'll never find it. Then once our rescuers arrive, we'll tell the police we had nothing to do with it. Even if they arrest me, I'll make bail, get your precious bribe money —"

Mr. Ober said, "Bribe?"

"Heh," the old man said. "Why I never go in one of these things if I don't have to. I do safety inspections."

Mr. and Mrs. Jackson glanced at each other, and Mrs. Jackson wondered what "safety issues" the greenhouse they just went into had.

Pearl acted as though she hadn't been interrupted. "— and be out of the country the next day." She clicked her tongue.

The clicking of the guns that cold night under the blazing moonlight as their hammers were pulled back had warned her.

Pearl laughed. "Plus you have no proof. My lawyers already have enough on each one of you here to discredit you to any jury in the world."

The rest looked at each other, dismayed. But Mrs. Jackson's mind was entirely on that cold moon-lit night, back in the place she'd known so well.

When the gun raised against the man she loved, she'd jumped in front of him. The scar on her arm would be there until the day she died.

I was ready to die, she realized. Nothing had been more important than for him and their little son to be alive, safe and free.

But even putting herself in front of the bullets had failed: he lay dead anyway.

*What else could I have **done**?*

The answer came. Her Mr. Jackson had said it, a few hours before: *You did the best you possibly could!*

Just like these girls, she'd done everything she could have. But she'd never believed it until now.

Mr. Jackson put his arm round her, and she leaned on his shoulder, feeling moved.

She'd done everything she could.

She still loved her first husband desperately. She still grieved his death fiercely. But no matter what happened next, even if the men hunting her caught and killed her tonight, she was free from that terrible guilt.

She was free.

An older man's voice came from behind. "Just like the last time."

Millie let out a yelp.

The group turned towards the man's voice.

Sergeant Nestor stood there.

18

Mrs. Jackson felt annoyed. "Good grief. How long have **you** been standing there?"

"Long enough." The sergeant had a dozen police with him, as well as the Hotel's maintenance man Eugene, who held a key. Sergeant Nestor pointed at the twins. "Don't let these two fool you."

Then he pointed back, into the darkness around the pool. "It's okay," he called out. "You can get the poor lad now." He pointed at Ruby and Pearl. "These two murdered his roommate, then did the same trick as they're trying now. The unsuspecting innocent gymnastics star —"

Mr. Jackson blurted out, "So **that's** how they had such balance with those ladders!"

Sergeant Nestor seemed not have heard. " — and her horrible twin. Which was which? They even confused the judge! So much so that they never saw a day in jail. I say you're both under arrest." He turned to his officers. "Cuff 'em, boys."

Pearl laughed as the officers forced her to her feet. "You have no proof!"

Sergeant Nestor said, "We have a dozen officers who just heard you confess. I'm sure we can find some evidence this time. For example, the Veronal in the boy's system. How did you manage to get him into the pool?"

All round went murmurs of "Yeah!" and "I'd sure like to know."

Ruby looked abashed. "He was only half awake. We used to swim together after school, and I told him it was time for practice. He never really understood what was happening until the end there."

Victor said, "Shame on you! I hope you both hang!"

Mrs. Jackson said to the twins, "Did killing Mr. Rothman make any of it better?"

Pearl rolled her eyes.

Ruby began to cry. "No."

Like her, these two girls had lost everything, even the man they loved. But instead of finding a new life, they'd turned their grief into a lust for revenge. "There's one thing I don't understand. Why kill Hugh's roommate? What was he to you?"

"Heh," Pearl said. "He was Mrs. Von Bilten's lookout man. He'd find out when the shows were to take place. He got a nice fee for sneaking the boys into the show."

Cornelius Ober's mouth fell open. "So **that's** how she did it."

"You'll never pin that one on us," Pearl said. "Double jeopardy."

Four of the sergeant's young officers led the two young women off. The five musicians began packing up their things.

Mrs. Jackson said, "This explains the splashing."

Sergeant Nestor said, "What's that?"

"One thing has bothered me," Mrs. Jackson said. "A champion swimmer would surely know how to keep himself from drowning, even if deeply intoxicated. And then there was Ruby's story. She said she saw the waiter floating. His white shirt startled her! She then went in to help him, but couldn't reach him. Then she called for aid. That was the story. But I was in the toilet not ten feet away. I heard a great deal of splashing for at least a minute. Then her footsteps, then she shrieked and called for help not a second later. And her dress was dripping! That's what made no sense. From the time of her shriek to calling for help, she should've been in the pool if she really were trying to help him. Or out of it with her dress dry. Not out of it soaking wet!" She shook her head. "That woman had to have murdered the man."

If only she'd gone out when the splashing began ...

But how was she to know?

"Too bad I can't put you on the stand," Sergeant Nestor said. "That'd make for some good testimony."

"I know," Mrs. Jackson said sadly. "And I'm sorry for that. I appreciate your care of us, I truly do."

The sergeant said quietly, "That reporter over there's been filling notebooks, and I'm sure the photographer hasn't been idle either. I think we got enough."

Eugene handed an envelope to Mr. Jackson, "A telegram came for you before the lights went out. The front desk is a madhouse, but since I was coming up, they gave it to me. It says it's urgent."

At that moment, George Neuberg and Ophelia Denton burst through the door to the stairs. Ophelia cried out, "You're safe!"

Mrs. Jackson stood, amused. "We are!"

Ophelia flew into her arms, sobbing. "You're safe. You're safe."

Mrs. Jackson smoothed her hair. "My dear little Pet. All's well."

George panted, "We heard someone was dead up here, and ..."

Mr. Jackson smiled fondly at George. "We're perfectly well. Although two others aren't so."

"I'm sorry," Ophelia said to Mrs. Jackson. "I should never have pushed you to talk."

Sergeant Nestor said, "Make that three. Well, I guess I should say five." He called out, "Lewis McKenney, you're under arrest for accepting bribes."

The old man said, "What?"

"Heard it from your own mouth," the sergeant said. "And the money's around here somewhere."

Mrs. Jackson smiled at Ophelia, put her arm around her shoulders, and kissed her forehead, feeling moved. "I forgive you."

The old man grumbled, "All I wanted was to retire."

"Well, you did it the wrong way," the sergeant said. "Go ahead and take him."

As the old man was taken off in handcuffs, George turned to Ophelia. "Look how lovely it is up here!"

Ophelia looked up, wiping her eyes. "Gosh ... it is! You can see the sky ever so well. And the torches, and candles." Her face glowed. "It's quite romantic."

George grinned. "I thought so too." He took Ophelia's hands, going to one knee in front of everyone. "Ophie, nothing would please me more than to spend the rest of our lives together. Will you marry me?" He looked uncertain. "I don't have a ring for you yet, but you can pick out anything you like."

Ophelia beamed. "I think that would be wonderful."

He threw his arms around her. "Then it's settled!"

Everyone standing around broke into applause.

Mr. and Mrs. Jackson looked at each other in wonder.

Mr. Jackson said, "I ... never thought **this** would happen!"

George said to him, "You're not sore, are you?"

"Astonished is more the word for it." He gave George a quick strong hug, then pulled away. "But I agree, this is perfect." He beamed at Ophelia. "For you both."

Mrs. Jackson said, "I entirely agree."

Cornelius Ober had been watching the scene, looking at George, then at Mr. Jackson. He came up to Mr. Jackson and offered his hand. "Have you ever been to Towertown? I know of a club there that I think you and your friends would very much enjoy."

George seemed surprised.

Mr. Jackson grinned at Mr. Ober, shifting the telegram to his left hand to shake the man's hand. "I've never been, sir, but I'd be glad to visit with you."

Amused, Mr. Ober went to Millie and said, "I do believe you were right!"

"I always know these things," she took his arm, and the two headed for the drink table. "Want to go dancing?"

Mr. Jackson opened the telegram, read it. Then he looked happier than Mrs. Jackson had ever seen him. "I have excellent news."

At once, Mrs. Jackson knew. "They accepted your offer on the property!"

"So they did." Mr. Jackson said. He put his arms over George and Ophelia's shoulder. "We have a lot of planning to do!"

"We sure do," George said. "I've got a wedding to plan!"

Ophelia began to laugh.

Mr. and Mrs. Jackson looked at each other, and he smiled. She said to them, "And we'll tell you where it is. Everything about it."

Ophelia's eyes filled with tears, and both she and George hugged Mrs. Jackson, making a perfect square. "We won't make you regret it," George said.

And Mrs. Jackson felt such tenderness for these two, making their way in a place that didn't understand them, that she kissed each of them on the cheek in turn.

Ophelia looked up at George. "You know, I'll make a terrible wife — I can't clean worth beans."

Mrs. Jackson looked across at her Mr. Jackson, who had a wry smile on his face.

George laughed. "Me either. But don't worry: we'll learn together."

Epilogue

Pearl Carlisle was charged with the premeditated murder of Horace Rothmore. Her sister Ruby Carlisle was charged with being an accomplice after the fact. Ruby was also charged with the premeditated murder of Hugh Portman.

With the testimonies of over a dozen police and the several notable citizens in attendance, the twins were both found guilty and sentenced to prison.

Lewis McKenney was charged with receiving bribes. The money was found — on the landing over the side — and seized by the city. However, Mr. Carlo made a deal with Mr. McKenney: tell me how to fix my greenhouse, and I'll do what I can to help. They came to a suitable arrangement.

Walter Margin turned over the photo of the architect speaking with the boys to the police. The elevator-men at the Myriad Hotel confirmed these boys were the ones who'd been riding the day the Myriad greenhouse panes were broken. The boys were charged with multiple counts of vandalism and sent to delinquency school.

Lydia Von Bilten was charged with inciting vandalism. In light of these crimes indirectly leading to her only son's death, the charges were dropped. The old lady was warned not to approach those children again, nor to incite any further mischief, or she would be jailed.

But Bence Gereben's notes became the story of the hour: Lydia Rothmore Von Bilten, the secret bankroller to her murdered love child! After a storm of scandal, she eventually moved away in disgrace.

Charles De Rege and Cornelius Ober struck up a friendship, and after some time, Charles decided to pursue a theatrical career.

George Neuberg's parents were delighted to hear of his engagement! After much thought during his two-week suspension for leaving his post, George reapplied for the front manager position at the Myriad Hotel and was accepted.

Will immediately stepped into the Headwaiter position he'd been training for, staying at the job for some time.

Club Patruni was not pleased to hear they'd be losing one of their showgirls. But Ophelia decided to apprentice with the costume department, and was soon happily sewing on beads and sequins for the show's next line-up.

Her friend Ethel's mother set her up with a young man who'd admired her from afar for some time. The pair hit it off!

Mrs. Kilpatrick was most relieved to hear that Ophelia and George were to be married. "I knew that young man would propose." She offered to make Ophelia's veil.

Mr. Jackson soon had the blueprints for his new property, and the two couples spent many happy hours talking about what he might do with the place.

Mrs. Jackson made arrangements to have Bessie visit her pups on a regular basis. This was most satisfactory to all parties involved.

Ophelia, George, Mrs. Jackson, Mr. Jackson, and Bessie went to the jewelry shop to pick out Ophelia's engagement ring.

Ophelia gasped when she saw it: a raised band of gold with a beautifully cut topaz gem. "It's perfect."

The next book in the Myriad Mysteries is coming soon!

To learn more about the Myriad Mysteries,
visit AuthorClaireLogan.com.

Sign up to my newsletter at
news.authorclairelogan.com

Acknowledgements

Thanks so much to Patricia Loofbourrow for the cover design. Also, thanks to Rebekah Brown for beta reading, and to my newsletter readers for providing names for this series — as well as picking out the location for the mysteries in this book!

Vote on where the next mysteries will occur at
vote.authorclairelogan.com

About the Author

I've loved reading since I can remember! I love puzzles and mysteries and intrigue, and of all the cities I've been to, Chicago is my favorite. My four years living in Chicago during grad school were wonderful. Plus I love history. And wasn't the 1920's wild? I've always wanted to write a fun mystery series set in Chicago and now here's my chance.

Claire Logan is a pen name.